Green with Envy

Nichole Ruschelle

To anyone who loves or wants to be called princess.

Note to Readers

Thank you so much for picking up this book and reading it.

This book is a fun twisted look at the fairy tale The Frog Prince. This story is based off of The Brothers Grimm version.

Contents

Chapter One

Brendan

Gripping my cigarette a little harder than necessary, I take a drag filling up my lungs with nicotine and trying to convince my body to relax. Not that it works. The day I've waited for but dreaded is here. Suri Jones, back from her self-appointed exile. She left four years ago to get her degree. She always does what's expected of her like a good little princess.

I'm not sure why I'm here... watching. For some reason, I needed to see her. I needed to punish myself. She looks the same as I've pictured her in my dreams over the years but I can't seem to forget the night she shattered my world.

That night plays over and over in my mind. *Standing on the balcony together, getting ready to profess my love to her, but before I can even get the words out she blurts, "Brendan, I'm engaged to your brother. When I graduate college, I'm going to marry him. It's what's best for my family."*

A car door slams and my head whips to the driveway. I see her foot first with one of those strappy sandals that she loves and I can't tear my eyes away from her seriously long legs. As she folds herself out of the car, my breath stalls and my jaw clenches. Fuck...she's even more stunning than I remember. Her curves seem fuller encased in those cut offs and a shirt that leaves nothing to the imagination. Her hair grazes her shoulder. She licks her lips...

Well fuck. Standing here staring at her, my cock starts to take notice. Technically she belongs to my brother. But only one word comes to mind when I look at her. Mine.

I shake my head. This will be messy. Complicated. But Suri will be mine. Deep down I know she feels the same but fear and obligation keep her in line. I need a plan. A surefire way to get the girl without letting anyone get in our way.

The memories of her telling me about being engaged try to run rampant through my brain. Her angelic voice ringing in my ears, *"Brendan, we were never supposed to be together. I'm destined for bigger things than you. This is something I have to do."*

"Bullshit," I whisper. Great, now I'm talking to myself like a pussy. What the fuck is wrong with me. Suri...she does this to me. Makes me crazy.

A dull throb starts to take flight in my chest. I take another drag of my cigarette but it does nothing. My lungs feel like they can't get enough air. We always talked about the future and getting married. She never cared about the pretenses of our family's expectations.

I know her stepmother orchestrated the engagement to my brother. The whole thing just pisses me off. Making matters worse, I saw her after the gala. Holding hands. Smiling. She looked stiff and the smile didn't reach her eyes, and Kieran's eyes kept roaming around the room never focusing on her. But that didn't stop the jealousy from swirling low in my stomach.

Clenching my fists around the pack of cigarettes, I crush them. While Suri has been away preparing herself for marriage, my brother has been off fucking his way through the city. I overheard him bragging to Henry how he loves to check out the auctions. It disgusts me to think that he has the most precious thing in his possession, and doesn't even care.

Looking at her now my eyes take in her glowing dark skin, flawless as always. Her gorgeous ass fills out her jean shorts and makes me want to march over there and spank it. Make it sting so that every time she goes to sit down she remembers that she belongs to me.

I bet she still tastes like coconuts. Maybe I'll run my tongue up and down her legs to find out. The sun hits the cleavage spilling from her halter top and I can see the outline of her perfect breasts. My hands start to twitch with the need to grab them. I have never met a woman more beautiful than Suri. Since I first laid eyes on her when we were kids, I knew she was it for me. Quiet. Reserved. Shy almost. She has no idea the effect she has on men. Wearing shorts and tennis shoes, face clear of makeup, I can't take my eyes off her. We never did much more than kissing before she left. She was young and not ready. Now...all bets are off.

Finishing the last drag of my cigarette, I throw it on the ground and grind it out with my shoe. Concentrating on the cigarette butt, I try not to think about how she would feel underneath me, writhing with pleasure. I can feel my cock straining against my zipper. Shit, I need to leave before I go after her right now. I'm not supposed to be here. I need a plan before I fuck this all up for a second time.

My father will kick my ass if he finds me here. He made a deal regarding my brother and Suri and my dad never backs out of a deal. His decisions revolve around power, class, order and money, not the desires of his second born spare.

My phone starts to vibrate in my back pocket, bringing me out of the trance that she seems to have me in. I look down as I pull it out, and see that it's the devil himself, my father. He's got quite the sixth sense. I hit accept "Yeah."

My father's voice fills the air when he grunts out, "Where are you?"

I can't let him know where I'm at so I keep it vague. "I'm out."

He hums, "Get to the warehouse. We need to talk."

I just grunt, hanging up the phone. As hard as it is to pull myself away, I get back into my car. Throwing my phone down in the passenger seat next to me, I don't look back. I just keep moving forward.

It won't be long before I never have to secretly drive away from her again.

Pulling up to the warehouse, I see Kieran standing next to my dad. Our men hustle all around them, taking orders from Henry, orders that Da and Kieran had passed along to him.

My brother and I are complete opposites. He takes after my father while I look more like our mother. He has light hair with green eyes and I have dark hair with blue eyes. We're both tall, but where he's toned and lean, I'm more filled with muscle. A must in my job within the family. I need to be strong, look imposing to our enemies, and I was bred to protect the family at all costs. He runs the family businesses. I know he thinks I'm only good for getting into fights. The brains and the muscle - or so my family believes. They treat me like the hired help without any skills or knowledge of the business side of things. My whole life has revolved around my look, my image, my brawn. Deep down I know my worth but that's not to say it doesn't get to me sometimes.

My brother and father have their heads down talking in whispers. Conspiring about something I'm sure. I can tell it's serious because my father seems tense. Something bad must have happened for them to bring me in. They only need me when there's trouble. The sacrificial lamb. The second son, not the heir, just the spare, as my brother likes to remind me. Neither one of them would be caught getting their hands dirty. But mine? No problem. I can't fight Da. If I dare to defy him then he will cast me out, not just out of the organization, but out of the family. I would never be able to contact my brother or mother again. It would break her heart.

I push open the car door and get out. When the door slams, they both look up at me.

Nodding my head to show the respect their positions grant them, I say, "Hello Da, Kieran."

Putting my hands in my pockets, I stop right in front of them. I don't say anything and let the silence fester. Most people can't help but fill the silence and in my line of work, in this family, I use it to my advantage.

Finally, my brother rolls his eyes. He glances over to Henry who is standing behind them, nodding his head, to indicate that Henry should join us. Once Henry joins, he finally speaks. "Brendan, we have a job for you. Sean from the butcher store doesn't want to pay what he owes us. I need you and Henry to go make sure they know that the O'Sullivan's are in charge."

He passes me a paper with the address on it. I take a deep breath and move my eyes away from my brother to the head of our family. "Da, why are you sending us to do this? We have men who could shake him down?"

His hardened eyes settle on me, he points his fingers at me with a deep growl. "You need to remember your place and do as I say."

I just shrug my shoulders, not wanting them to know that by not answering my question, I'm even more curious. Placing the paper in my pocket, I huff out, "Fine."

I look over at my best friend, Henry, "Let's go." Turning my back on my father and brother, I return to my car as Henry climbs into the passenger seat. We don't speak to each other, both inside our heads trying to figure out why we would be sent to enforce such small debts.

As we are driving Henry must decide to ask the question that's been on both of our minds. "Why do you think they're sending us to collect this payment?"

I shrug my shoulders and then refocus on the road ahead. "Who knows? Kieran and my father don't explain anything to me. But I saw Suri today, so I need the outlet and something to keep me away from her."

Henry sighs and returns to looking at the road. If he has any thoughts about me seeing Suri, he keeps them to himself.

Chapter Two

Suri

My heartbeat thunders in my chest as I sit here in the car. The car headed to the end of my life. A little dramatic I know but that's how it feels. The closer we get to my father's mansion, the more I feel the metaphorical bars of my jail cell closing around me. I knew this day would come, I just didn't think it would come so fast.

The tiny amount of freedom I've had over the last four years has vanished. I know I should be grateful that my father and stepmother allowed me to have that time, but it wasn't enough.

The driver turns the corner and I see the gate of the mansion ahead. My breaths start to pick up and my chest constricts so tightly I start to panic. I need to get myself together. If I want to survive, I need to be strong.

Remembering the technique that my best friend Ella taught me to help calm myself down, I close my eyes tightly and count to ten. Taking a deep breath, I concentrate on how the air fills my lungs. I hold it in and then release it as I count backward from ten. My breathing starts to instantly calm. I continue to think about all of the good things in my life. *I'll be ok. I have a friend who cares about me.*

The thought of Ella makes me smile. I met her junior year in high school and we have been inseparable ever since. She was my only friend other than Brendan and Henry. I spent most of my time with Brendan. I'd never cared to waste my time with anyone else.

I remind myself of more good things as we get closer to the house. *I'm almost done with my book, and I just graduated with a degree in creative writing. These are all accomplishments that I achieved. No one can take them away from me.*

Keeping my eyes closed, I take another deep breath counting backward and forward from ten. As I'm counting my blessings, I hear the noise of a throat clearing.

"Ma'am."

Ignoring the driver, I take one last breath. As I'm letting it out, I hear him again. "Uh...Ma'am."

Knowing he won't stop unless I acknowledge him, I slowly open my eyes. He tries again. "We're here. Ma'am."

I gather my purse and get out of the car, whispering, "Sorry. Thank you for the ride."

My legs feel heavy as if they're made of lead. Forcing them to move, I make my way toward the front door. Thankfully, the driver helps bring my luggage up to the house. I apologize and thank him again before handing him a generous tip and walking through the front door.

One of the housekeepers comes through the living room cheerfully greeting me. "Hello Miss Suri, welcome home."

Looking around, my stomach drops. No one but the housekeeper is here to greet me. I don't know why I'm surprised. It's been like this since my father married Mallory.

My stepmother has always seen me as a nuisance. She ignores me for the most part, except for when she needs me to do something for her. She is a master manipulator. She always knows exactly how to hurt me, emotionally or physically.

I give her my best smile though we both know that it's fake. "Thank you, Ariana."

I take another breath. "You're fine, Suri," I mutter under my breath. Heading toward the stairs to retreat to my room, I decide to ask the question weighing on my mind. "Ariana, do you know where my father is?"

She looks at me with pity in her eyes. "Your father and Mallory are in the city for the night."

I hate that look on her face. I've been getting it ever since I was five. When my mother passed and he decided to marry a woman that doesn't want anything to do with me. He was the best father until her. Now he just does what he can do to keep her happy. Meaning he forgets about me. I need to get away from it. Pushing my curls back away from my face, I whisper, "Thank you."

Walking into my room is like going back in time four years ago, a time when my future was changed with one simple deal. A deal I didn't make but yet broke my heart all the same.

My room reminds me of Brendan. So many countless hours we spent sitting on my bed, talking, laughing, planning. I loved being in my room until that final day.

Now, the memories start to assault me all at once like scenes in a movie. My father and Mallory entering my room, telling me we have to talk. The sinister smile on Mallory's face...

I should've known it would be something terrible. That's when they dropped the bomb that I'll have to marry Kieran. Tears start to trail down my cheeks just like they did that night. The voice of my father echoes around the room.

"Suri, you will give up Brendan, for the good of the family. Kieran is the older brother and will take over for his family's business. Your marriage to him will ensure that we have power in the alliance between families."

At the time I couldn't even fathom the idea of giving up Brendan. I knew, and I still know, deep down that we are meant to be together. I argued with Mallory and my father but they stood their ground, reminding me of my duty to the family. I laid on my bed and cried. My father kissed my temple and left.

Then came Mallory's threat whispered in my ears under the guise of love and care. "If you don't marry Kieran, I will destroy your father and take everything away from you."

That ended the fight for me. No matter my circumstance, I loved my father. I never doubted Mallory's threats. She wants everything for herself and nothing for anyone else. At that moment, I knew I would let Brendan go and marry Kieran. It would be the hardest thing I ever did and I still wasn't sure I could go through with it.

Grabbing my phone, I text Ella needing a friend and a distraction.

> **Me:** Hey I'm home, but of course, the king and his witch aren't here.

> **Ella:** Glad you made it home safely. It's probably for the best that the witch isn't there. Where did they go?

Me: True. They are staying in the city for the night. I'm gonna take advantage of them being gone by catching up on Netflix. Do you want to come over and hang out?

Ella: I wish I could, but I have to work.

Me: That sucks. Maybe another time. Love you, have a good night.

Ella: Love you!

I put my phone on silent and place it in a drawer on my nightstand. Determined to not feel sorry for myself, I turn on Netflix and start to unpack while watching an episode of The Great British Bake Off.

Looking at the time, I realize I never ate dinner. It's getting late and my stomach rumbles. I turn off the TV and head down to the kitchen to find something to eat.

Ariana left me a plate of food in the fridge, so I heat it up and sit down to eat. Sitting by myself at home eating alone. No parents, no fiance, no friends. Most likely just like almost every night of my new life. Lonely. As I sit in the quiet, all I can think is that Brendan would be here if I asked. He always showed up for me...no questions asked. I just wished I could have him back.

Chapter Three

Brendan

Henry and I pull the car up outside of a rundown building. I check to make sure that I have the right address from the paper that Da gave us. It's an old butcher shop and the owner has been avoiding the debt collectors. He knew what would happen if he refused to pay...so today he gets me.

The sun has gone down. It's easier to take cover in the dark. I belong in the darkness. My father made that clear to me a long time ago. I think that's why I'm so drawn to Suri; she's always been a sparkle of light for me. The light to my dark even though she may be the only person in my life who never actually saw my darkness. She always knew exactly how to calm me, just a simple touch, when it threatened to consume me. Leading me out of the tunnel toward the light. Her confidence in me, making me feel like I could do anything.

"Hey, boss. You ok over there?" Henry says, interrupting my thoughts.

"Yeah man, sorry. You ready for this?" I ask as I flex my fist.

"Yep. Let's get this over with."

As we get out of the car, I turn to make eye contact with Henry and he nods. Henry and I have done this dance so many times that we know exactly what to do. I head toward the front door while he makes his way to the back of the building.

A middle-aged man stands behind the counter. He looks up and we make eye contact, his eyes going wide. He knows exactly why I'm here. He starts to run. Damn it! *Why do they always run? I hate it when they run. It makes my life so much harder. If they borrow money from someone like my father, pay up or suffer the consequences like a man!*

He doesn't make it very far when a punch to the face from Henry takes him down. I grab him by his collar and lift him to his feet. He has blood running down his face and looks scared shitless. Leaning in close, I sneer at him "Fuck, Sean, why did you have to go and do that? Now I have to punish you for not paying and add extra for trying to take off. We can't have people thinking that you can run from the O'Sullivans."

I release him and he falls to the ground. I stand up to my full height and deliver a brutal kick to his ribs. "Sean, my money?"

He gasps trying to breathe as he sputters out, "I don't have it."

"Tsk tsk. Not the answer I want to hear, Sean."

I grab my knife from inside my suit jacket. "Grab his hand."

Henry secures Sean's hand because what I'm about to do will hurt like a bitch. Sean's eyes get large as realization sets in and he screams,

"No! Fuck no. I'll do anything. Please!"

Moving closer, I take his hand from Henry and look Sean dead in the eyes. "Next time you want to run from me, you'll think twice. I will be back in one week and you better have my money. I have no problem taking everything away from you. And I mean everything. Your business, your wife, kids"....glancing down at his hand that I'm about to take the finger from. "Do you understand?"

I don't wait for an answer. I take what is owed to me. I slice off his ring finger and we watch his wedding ring roll across the floor. I stand up, straightening my suit. Sean screams in the background. Maybe from losing his finger or maybe it's the threat of what I might do next. Who knows? Men like him are weak. They give into their addictions without giving any thought to the impact on others. He borrowed a ridiculous amount of money from the mafia so he could gamble and drink his life away. He didn't care that we'd go after his family and business.

Henry and I leave out the front door. "What did you mean you would take away his wife and kids? You know we don't hurt families."

I take a deep breath. "You and I know that, but he doesn't. Plus, I would take away his kids and wife. I would make sure they know that he's a piece of shit, give them some money, and then kill him."

Henry chuckles and slaps his hand on my shoulder "So true, my man. He is a piece of shit."

Both grinning, we get in the car and I put it in drive. I head toward the apartment building that Henry and I both live in. We like to stay close to each other in case we have to go out in the middle of the night.

Taking the elevator up to my apartment, I text my Da that I've taken care of the job. I put my phone on silent. I'm done for the night. I don't want to talk to anyone or be interrupted again. After pouring myself a whiskey from the drink cart in the corner of the living room, I walk over to the floor to ceiling windows and look out over the city. This view always gives me a sense of calm. It reminds me of how small we all are. The world might be full of crazy shit, but there is more out there. Good things. Beautiful things.

Like Suri.

I used to love our late-night talks when we were younger. In the dark and quiet, I always miss her the most. I hate that I can't seem to get her out of my mind. I tap my fingers on my temple as if I will be able to knock out the memories of us together but they don't ever leave me. They just haunt me.

So much for fucking sleep.

Grabbing my car keys, I head toward the elevator. The need to see Suri is overwhelming. I park my car outside of her house and just wait...staring. Darkness looms over the mansion and it seems quiet. I absentmindedly make my way to the fence on the side of the house that faces the opposite side of the street. I've done this before so I know the best way to get to her window.

Reaching the house, I see the lattice that leads up to her window. With no lights on in her room, I assume she's asleep. The perfect time to get in without her knowing. I climb the lattice and am surprised that I can easily lift the window. Has she been waiting for me? Sitting on her windowsill watching her sleep, I let myself hope. Hope she thinks about me as much as I do her. Hope she still wants me like I want her. And I fucking hope to God she wants to walk away from my brother and possibly our families. She belongs to me and it's time I get her back.

She looks so peaceful. I walk over to her and my fingers twitch. I know it's a bad idea but I need to touch her. I rub my fingers over her beautiful high cheekbones, hoping she still sleeps as deeply as when we were kids. Her skin feels so warm along the path that I take with my finger tips. Letting out a small moan, she leans into me. I can see her eyes fluttering under her lids. What are you dreaming about, princess?

No one has ever been able to get my attention like Suri. I've tried to forget her. I've tried to move on. Her tongue slowly swipes along her bottom lip. My eyes follow the movement. Her luscious lips so plump, I lean down and brush my lips over hers. It's taking everything in me to resist the urge to deepen the kiss. Her hand moves and I notice that she doesn't have on her ring. I swear she doesn't want to marry my brother. She wants to be with me. It's always been me and her.

"Don't worry, princess. I vow right here, right now, that I will be the man you marry," I whisper in her ear.

I lay down next to her and wrap my arms around her pulling her as close to me as possible without disturbing her. She snuggles more into me, laying her head down over my heart. Her hand comes up, gripping my shirt as if her subconscious knows that she is safe. Resting my chin on top of her head I don't dare move. Not now that I'm holding Suri again...finally. It feels so right. So perfect.

I have to talk to my brother, figure out once and for all what he feels for her if anything. I have to tell him and Da how I'm feeling and what I want. I might lose everything. My family. My job. But if I have Suri, I just don't fucking care anymore. Her contented sighs, her body pressed to mine, and her little fist keeping close tells me she feels the same way. As the sun starts to peek through the night sky, I know it's time to leave. For now. Gathering up all my strength I stand up and walk toward the window.

Looking back at her, my heart starts to race. I don't like the thought of leaving her, but I know what I need to do. I will give everything up for her.

Our future starts today, she just doesn't know it yet.

Chapter Four

Suri

B am!! The door swings open and hits the wall, suddenly waking me up. Before I can even register what is occurring I hear her, "Get up! Why do you have to be so lazy? It's time to get up"

Looking over at my alarm clock I can see that it's noon, but darn it I deserve to sleep in. I've been working non-stop for the last four years to earn my degree. Plus working on my very own book. I roll my eyes at Mallory's antics, simultaneously pulling the covers up over my head, trying to ignore her. That's when I smell him, was he here yesterday? I try to think back to my memories. I know that I dreamed about him being here with me...Suddenly the covers are ripped from me and all I see is her standing over me sneering, as she yells "Get up now Suri!"

Her voice seemed to go up an octave, causing me to wince. Shit, this isn't good. Standing up from the bed, "Fine. I'm getting up."

I go to move to the bathroom, but Mallory blocks my way, her face shows that she is displeased with me. Fuck how did I already piss her off, I just got home yesterday. Mallory finally breaks the stand-off with me, leaning in and whispering "Suri you listen to me you spoiled brat. You need to get ready, we have dinner tonight with Kieran and his family. Don't embarrass me."

I'm not sure how my father even deals with her, she is so selfish. She has never been a big fan of me. Even when I was younger, she treated me with such disdain of course only in private. In front of my father, she would only muster up indifference, but that was fine with my father. He didn't need anyone to give me motherly attention; we had nannies for that. Once my mother died, my father turned into a different person. He left me behind.

I just stare at her, as the loneliness of life starts to seep through. This woman has taken everything from me for selfish reasons. Her lips flatten knowing she isn't going to get much from me. "I will see you downstairs in an hour, we will go to the store to pick out a suitable dress for dinner."

Nodding, I take that as a cue that our conversation is finished. I move past her and enter the bathroom, shutting the door. I make sure to take my time getting dressed. I make it down the stairs, right at the one-hour mark. Where I find Mallory standing with a scowl on her face. Which deepens as soon as she sees me. "Let's go. I don't want to have to be out with you longer than necessary."

Ten minutes later we pull up in front of an upscale boutique. Releasing a breath I follow Mallory out of the car and into the boutique. I just want to get a dress and get back, so I don't have to be near this witch longer than necessary. I already have a plan that I'm going to follow in my head. I'm just gonna accept whatever dress she picks out and just wear it. I just want to get this day over.

As we enter we are met by a thin blonde lady, she hands a glass of champagne over to Mallory. She looks me up and down with a critical eye before she returns them to the witch, "What can I do for you today?"

Taking a sip of her champagne before answering, Mallory politely responds in a way that I didn't know was possible "We need a dress for my step-daughter, we are having dinner with her fiance tonight."

We move more into the store, where I spot a couch, I move over to it and sit down crossing my legs. Then I hear her screechy voice "What are you doing?"

"You seem like you already know what you would like me to wear, I will put on whatever you pick," I say with such a cool tone, I don't want her to know that all of this angers me. Taking my choices away from me, as I don't have any thoughts of my own. I'm sure she knows since I've let it be known to my father how I feel since the night he told me about the engagement.

She just scoffs and rolls her eyes, moving towards a rack of dresses. I feel a little bit relieved the farther away from me she gets. I can't stand that woman, I'm not sure how much more I can take. After ten minutes the attendant in the store comes up "We have a dressing room ready for you."

Staying silent I get up without any complaint and move to the dressing room. The stack of dresses hanging up, are gorgeous, I move closer to get a better look at them. They are really beautiful, too bad such beautiful things will be sullied by the act of forced marriage. My thoughts start to daydream about a different life, but I push those away. I don't have a different life, this is my life. Engaged to the brother of the man that I want to be with, to ensure that my family stays on top.

Grabbing the first dress a little too aggressively, I put it on, and it's a simple black sheath dress. It compliments my skin tone and seems to be fine, nothing to fancy. Not putting too much thought into it, I change back into my clothes, walking out I let the consultant know that this is the one I'll be taking. She nods, walking back into the store, I shout "Mallory I've picked one. I will be on the couch."

She doesn't respond. Of course, there is no response. Why would she want to be decent and answer me? I sit down on the couch, pulling out my phone. My neck starts to tingle, and it moves down my spine causing my whole body to feel as if it's been electrocuted. I know that feeling. It's the one I get every time he is near. I love and hate the way my body reacts when he's close. It kills me that we have to stay apart. I try not to fidget or look around, I don't want him to know that I realize he is near.

Chapter Five

Brendan

Entering Suri's house for the first time in years without sneaking in feels surreal. I never liked this place. It brings back feelings of secrecy and uncomfortableness. Suri's stepmother always had a knack for making me feel small to the point I'd feel uneasy in my skin. It led to me sneaking into the house just to avoid any side comments from her.

Funnily enough, Suri's parents forcing her into this engagement with my brother helped me grow into the man I am today. More confident, more sure of myself, and more cold. I used to allow my emotions to get the best of me. Reacting before thinking about the best way to handle situations. Now I have more self-discipline than even my Da would like me to have.

As we stand in the foyer being greeted by the housekeeper, my body tenses knowing that I'll see her soon. My Da, Ma, Kieran and I are all here to discuss the finer points of their engagement. Apparently we all have to be here to show that we stand as one, but I'm just here to get a glimpse of her.

I start to zone out because honestly I would rather have Henry torture me and pluck my eyes out than listen to this crap. My family moves deeper into the house, but I can't seem to command my body to follow. I can feel my lips start to frown. Da must see it too because he quickly turns, pointing his finger at me. "Brendan, you *will* behave tonight. I will not have you jeopardize this engagement. You hear me?"

I don't answer him quickly enough so he slaps me upside my head. "I said did you hear me, Brendan?"

Sighing and rubbing the back of my head, I answer, "Yes Da, I heard you. You don't have to hit me." *I make sure I school my face because I'm not ready for him to know that I don't plan on letting Suri marry Kieran. Even if I have to run away with her.*

He glares at me a beat longer but must be satisfied with whatever he sees on my face because he nods and turns back toward the housekeeper.

"Let's go," my Da mutters as he straightens his suit jacket.

The housekeeper turns and leads us into the gaudy black and gold sitting room. A high-pitched voice wraps around me and I hear the evil witch, the nickname Suri and I gave her as kids. "Brian, Maeve, welcome to our home. We're excited to have you here to discuss the two lovebirds."

She is so fucking full of it. We all know this is an arranged marriage. We don't have to talk as if they're in love. Shit, it's going to be a long night.

I make my way over to the couch and as I'm sitting down, I feel her. I know she's in the room before my eyes find her. They lock onto her and move down her body. I can't take my eyes off her no matter how hard I try. She's fucking gorgeous.

A beautiful black dress that hugs her in all the right places wraps around her body. I want to unwrap her and caress her dark smooth skin. I want to lick between her perfect, perky tits. I want her long lean legs wrapped around my neck as I lick her pussy. I drag my eyes back up her body to the storm of emotions brewing in her brown eyes.

I wish I could tell what she's thinking. I know she doesn't want this engagement despite what she tells me or herself. Does she still love me as much as I love her?

And I do love her, but as much as I love her, I also hate her. Well, I don't hate her but I hate what she does to me. I hate that even after all these years I can't stop thinking about her. And most of all I hate that she is willing to go through this facade of a marriage to my brother. I hate that I still hear those words especially when I'm at my weakest.

"I'm going to marry your brother."

Everyone is engaged in conversation around me but I can't seem to concentrate on anything. My body starts to feel antsy. I look up at her and her deep chocolate brown beautiful eyes glisten with unshed tears, holding an underlying sadness and loneliness to them. I want to gather her up and take away that look. Turning my head, I break her gaze and try to focus on the others.

The evil witch Mallory turns to me with a glint in her eye. She asks, "Brendan, what are you up to these days?"

Without missing a beat, I respond, "I'm head of security."

If she thinks that she's going to make me feel bad about anything in my life, she's wrong. I won't allow this woman to make me feel small anymore. I'm a grown ass adult. There was a time when she held this power over me, but not anymore. There was a time I convinced myself that if she liked me, she would realize that Suri and I should be together. But in the end, none of that mattered. I was never the right son.

She sighs, knowing that she didn't trip me up or get under my skin. Trying again, she smirks at me. I can tell that she thinks she's going to ask me something to rattle me. "Are you seeing anyone?"

"Mallory, that's none of your business," Richard booms.

She looks at her husband and shrugs. "I was curious. He's a good-looking man. Maybe he has a hooker that he's into?"

The room goes deadly silent. I can tell that my parents are not happy about the comments being made, but they won't say anything. They need this marriage to work as much as Mallory and Richard do. This marriage will make sure that my Da's business and Richard's intertwine even more than they already are.

"I don't have a specific whore that's mine, but do have a few on call," I say into the silence letting everyone know Mallory will not best me.

As I finish my words, I look at Suri. I see a flash of sadness and jealousy come across her face. I'm glad to see that she can feel something other than the numbness she projects. The fact that it's about me only makes the victory better. But I also feel like a dick. A lying sack of shit. I try to implore to her with my eyes that it isn't true but she keeps hers downcast on an imaginary speck on the floor.

Suri stands up quickly, smoothing her dress down. Her soft voice hits my ears. "Um, excuse me. I need to use the bathroom." She rushes out of the room quickly, never looking back.

Fuck.

My father clears his throat. I can tell by his body language that he wants to steer the conversation back to the marriage. "Shall we discuss the wedding now or do we need to wait for Suri?"

Mallory casually responds waving her hand in the air. "We can let Suri know later. She doesn't care about these things anyway."

With that remark, they start discussing a date for the wedding. My head starts to throb as the voices of the room all start talking at the same time. Needing to get away from this as quickly as possible, I get up to see where Suri went.

"Where are you going, Brendan?" Kieran asks.

I turn to him making sure he can't see the turmoil on my face. I see the suspicious look on his face as I mutter, "I'm going to smoke."

Walking down the hall, I take a detour away from the patio and head toward the bathroom, toward Suri. As I place my hand on the knob, the door suddenly yanks open. I see my opportunity and I take it.

"What are y-"

"Shh." I push her back into the bathroom before she can finish her protest. In the middle of the bathroom with my body up against hers, she looks at me with her mouth hanging open. I brush my lips over her ears whispering, "If you don't close your mouth, you might find my cock in it."

Those words seem to shake her out of her stupor and she sneers at me as she pushes against my chest, "What are you doing? We can't get caught together."

I don't let her push me away. I need her to feel it. The pull. The spark. The chemistry between us. I move my body to block her more.

I grab one of her curls and pull it down as I watch her chest heave and face flush. "We need to talk, princess."

Chapter Six

Suri

Frozen in time, I can't seem to move my body. Like I'm drugged with my body paralyzed but my mind reeling. Reeling at least a hundred miles a minute with the thoughts of Brendan, his cock, and my fiancé and family just down the hall. I'm just standing there with my mouth hanging open. Trapped between all kinds of right and wrong.

Snapping my jaw shut, I narrow my eyes at him and close my mouth as my body heats up from his words. I put my hands on his chest again and half-heartedly push against him as I stutter out, "P-please."

If I allow Brendan to get any closer, I won't be able to walk away from him. We can't be together, no matter how much we want it. Hell, I'm engaged to his brother! The ring on my finger gleams in the light reminding me of the responsibility that sits heavy on my shoulders.

I can feel the anger rolling off of him. Good I need his anger. Anything less will be unacceptable. He might think there's hope if he's not hating me. I lock my eyes with him straightening my shoulders and I snap, "We don't need to talk. You need to let me out of here."

I am surprised that my voice sounds so even and strong. Strong is not how I'm feeling right now. Brendan ghosts his lips over mine. My hands stay on his chest not sure if I'm trying to push him away or pull him closer. Before I can make up my mind, his lips crash down on mine.

He pushes down on them hard, punishing me. I suppose in a way he is. I'm the one who walked away from us. I can't stop my body from reacting. It has a mind of its own and it's always wanted Brendan. He brushes his hands up my sides causing my nipples to pebble with anticipation. Lightly brushing against each nipple, he keeps moving his hands up, tangling his hands into my hair. Getting lost in him, I open up my mouth giving him the access that he wants.

Grabbing the back of my neck, he pushes his tongue deeper into my mouth. He tastes like cinnamon and nicotine just like I remember. It's been four years but my body hasn't forgotten one bit of him. It's like no time has passed and forever has gone by in the same instant. My legs wrap around his waist as I pull myself into him, trying to get as close as possible. His hard cock rubbing against the outside of my panties, I can feel myself getting wetter. He starts to grind more into me when someone knocks on the door.

It's as if a bucket of cold water has been splashed on top of us. We pull away from each other as a second knock comes.

"Suri, what are you doing in there? You've been gone for a while," my Dad's deep voice calls through the door.

"Just a minute, Dad. I'm finishing up."

"Well, hurry up. We're waiting on you for dinner." I hear his footsteps getting farther away from the door. Not wanting to deal with the emotions that I have at the moment, I turn my back to Brendan.

I feel his breath on the shell of my ear when he whispers ,"You are mine, Suri, and I'm not going to allow you to marry my brother."

A feeling of deja vu comes over me as I gulp at his words. I look up into the mirror. His shoulders fill the mirror, his huge body surrounding mine making me feel small and safe. His hand brushes ever so lightly down my arm leaving goosebumps in its wake. He presses his shoulder and then the other, his eyes never leaving mine in the mirror. One lone tear falls down my cheek before he swipes it away with his finger. "Don't cry, princess. I'm going to fix this if it's the last thing I do. Be strong for me for just a little bit longer."

With one last look in the mirror, he leaves the bathroom. When I hear the click of the doorknob, my knees finally buckle. I give myself a moment before I turn myself into the strong girl he needs me to be. My shoulders sag. I look down at my hand and see my engagement ring. I can't help but wonder if Brendan will be able to marry me. Putting my mask back on, I can't help but wonder how long will it take before he's able to save me from this nightmare? Will we also be able to save my dad too?

Entering the dining room, I can feel the tension that fills the room heightening my anxiety. What the hell is going on? Why is everyone so tense? I hear Mallory call my name. I look up and see her waving me over, "Good, you're here, Suri. Come sit. We're just talking about the wedding. We're thinking spring. Will that work?"

I walk over to the table and sit in the only empty seat available next to Brendan and across from Kieran. A thought flashes through my mind, did Brendan sit like this on purpose? I mutter softly, "Spring is fine," as I pull my chair out trying not to make eye contact with Brendan.

I always imagined a summer wedding on the cliffs of Hawaii. Overlooking the beaches at sunset, but I don't bother to say that though because it doesn't matter. Mallory nods. "See? Nothing to worry about. Suri is very easygoing. A quality that will be perfect for a wife."

I roll my eyes at her words. They must have been arguing about the wedding. Before she can reprimand me, the doors to the kitchen open and the waiters dash into the room, bringing out dinner and placing it in front of us. I go to grab my fork when a hand caresses my thigh, causing me to gasp. "Suri, are you ok?" My dad asks.

"Oh, me, yes. Yes, of course. Just hungry and everything looks delicious." Brendan's hand squeezes gently, sending shockwaves straight to my clit.

"If you're sure. You look flushed."

"I'm sure. Please everyone eat." I lift one hand to my cheek trying to cool my skin. The other I slide under the table to link my fingers with Brendan's on my leg.

Brian's phone ringing cuts through the room. As he looks down, he scowls. His face smooths out though as he looks up. "I'm sorry, I have to take this call."

As he leaves the room, my dad tries to break up the silence. "How does everyone like their meal?"

Maeve gives him a small smile. She places her hand on his forearm speaking softly, "Oh it is great. You must give our compliments to the chef."

As soon as the words leave her mouth, Brian walks back into the room with no emotion on his face. He looks at my dad. "I'm sorry, but something has come up and we need to go." Moving his gaze to his sons, he barks, "Kieran, Brendan. Let's go."

Maeve and her sons briskly get up and leave us sitting at the dinner table. Once we hear the closing of the front door, my dad pushes back his seat. "Well, if you'll excuse me, I have some work to do in my office."

Mallory and I sit at the table silently. I place my fork down and start to excuse myself when she grabs my wrist with her hand, her nails digging into my skin. I try to pull away but she doesn't allow it. "Don't think I didn't see that you didn't even talk to Kieran," she hisses.

"He didn't talk to me either."

She lets go of me and speaks to me in an eerily calm voice. "You will marry him, Suri. I will not allow anyone to break up this engagement. Not you. Not Brendan. You know what will happen if you don't."

With those words, she turns and leaves me rubbing my wrist.

Shit, that one is going to bruise.

Chapter Seven

Brendan

Something must be going on for Da to have us leave dinner early. He harped on about how important it was, even going so far as telling those who work for him not to interrupt. So unless someone has a death wish, this must be an emergency.

Da pulls out of the driveway and starts to head toward our family home. He looks over at Ma. "Maeve, we're going to drop you off. Then the boys and I have to head to a meeting."

Ma just nods her head. She doesn't want to know what the meeting is about, which is for the best. The less she knows, the safer she'll be. Silence fills the car, all of us lost in our own thoughts about dinner and what's to come.

"Boys, we are heading to the warehouse. Some of our inventory is missing from the last shipment," Da explains after we drop Ma.

Neither of us speaks. I can feel the fury coming off of Da. I wonder who would be bold enough to steal from us. Pulling up to the warehouse, the tension feels palpable in the air. All of our men are standing around conversing with each other while they wait for instructions. Off to the side, Henry is talking with another man who is hidden in the shadows.

As we exit the car, every man stands at attention. Before anyone says anything, Henry moves in front of us, and I can finally see Zeev, who heads up the French Mafia with his wife Blanche. Zeev and my Da are part of a group of mafia men that support each other. They get together once a month to discuss pacts, strategies, and potential problems.

Zeev nods his head in respect and then says quietly, "Brian, we need to talk. I have some information."

"We'll talk in my office."

He and Zeev head toward the office leaving Kieran, Henry, and me behind.

I look over at Kieran and it just hits me. I need to talk to him. Now. I don't care about what's going on with the business. My priorities lie somewhere else. With someone else. And that's exactly why I'm not fit to be leading like Kieran. He cares for nothing but the business. I care for nothing but Suri.

I clear my throat not wanting to wait any longer. "Kieran, you need to tell Da that you won't marry Suri."

His look can only be described as shock. I guess he didn't think I'd bring it up. "You want to talk about this now, asshole, while somebody is messing with us and the business?"

I move closer to him, looking him square in the eyes so he can't misinterpret me. "Why the fuck not? I don't care about missing inventory. I care about getting back the only woman who's ever meant anything to me."

"I knew you still had feelings for her. Tell me, little brother... does it kill you that I'll be the one that will be sticking my dick in her instead of you?"

He wants a reaction out of me, and with the shit he's spewing, I'm willing to give it to him. I move quickly and cock my hand back but Kieran sees it coming. He moves out of the way causing me to miss his face, but I still get a good hit in on his shoulder.

"Fuck. That hurt, you asshole," he whines.

He rears back and moves to grab me, but I've always been better at fighting. He's so focused on trying to hit me that he doesn't see that I've backed him into a corner. Having nowhere to move, I'm able to get him in a headlock. I lean down and whisper so only he can hear me, "You will tell Da that you won't marry her."

Kieran moves and counteracts my headlock. He gets away from me and laughs before a serious look comes over his face. "Ok, Brendan, I'll talk to Da. I can't guarantee anything. You know how it is."

I let out a breath. "Thanks, brother."

Da may not agree, but it's a place to start. Maybe tonight will end up being the beginning of the rest of my life. Or maybe it will be the end.

Chapter Eight

Suri

A few days have passed since the crazy dinner with the O'Sullivans. One part of me keeps replaying my time with Brendan in the bathroom. Everytime my body heats up as the memories assault me. It was the hottest moment of my life...which isn't saying much .The other part of me can't stop thinking that he will never be mine. I can't have him without destroying my father. With so much at stake on both sides, I'm basically just a mess.

Trying to regain focus, I move back to my computer. I've been staring at it for days now. Reading and rereading the book I'm in the middle of writing. Nothing seems right. Everything I write down doesn't work. My thoughts stray to Brendan and Kieran. I place my hands over my face, trying to keep the feelings of anxiety at bay. What the fuck am I going to do?

It's obvious that Brendan isn't going to take this marriage sitting down, and honestly, I'm not sure that I want him to. The feelings I've had for him since we were kids are still there. I thought maybe I'd pushed them away, but after that dinner, it was very clear that I only repressed them.

I can tell Kieran doesn't want to marry me either, so maybe I can use that to my benefit. I don't want to be in a relationship with a man who doesn't even talk to me. I might've been able to convince myself if Kieran ever engaged with me. I shake my head knowing things may never change.

Does it matter though? For him maybe, but not for me. I know what's on the line here. Mallory won't let me get away without marrying Kieran. She's already informed me what she's willing to do to make sure she gets her way. I can't let my dad get hurt. Even though he hasn't been the same since my mom died, he's still my dad and I love him.

My phone buzzes on my nightstand. Ella's texting me and giving me a reason to smile. My best friend can always cheer me up.

Ella: Hey want to check out a new club tonight?

I take a deep breath and shrug thinking, why the hell not? It might be good to get away from all of this bullshit and have one night to just be me. Maybe it will give me some clarity for my life and the story I'm writing. And the bonus of the night: pissing Mallory off. She hates it when even my little toe veers outside the line of being perfect. And a nightclub....all the way outside the line.

Me: Yes! Let's do it.

Ella responds to me instantly, telling me that she will meet me at the new club, Midnight, around nine o'clock. Awesome, that gives me plenty of time to finish up this chapter in my book and get ready.

Knowing I am spending the evening with a friend must help me concentrate because I finish up the chapter of my book like I was hoping for. Feeling accomplished, I close my computer and head to the closet to get dressed for a night out. I look through all my outfits and decide to go with a classic black dress. It hugs my curves without looking like I'm trying too hard.

Walking into the bathroom to tame my wild curls as much as possible. Putting on light makeup, I look in the mirror and smile. Glancing at the clock, I rush to grab my purse and meet the driver downstairs. Climbing into the car, I get a feeling that tonight is going to be a good night.

The car pulls up to the club and I spot Ella right away.

"Hey stranger, it's been a long time since I've seen you," I say, hugging her tightly.

She lets out a sigh that sounds a bit defeated. "I know, I've been working a lot lately."

I clap my hands and give an exaggerated smile, "Let's go let off some steam."

Ella laughs, knowing that letting off steam is exactly what we both need. The club is amazing. The walls are a dark blue and the fixtures are silver giving it an expensive and elegant feel. Lights flash all through the club as bodies writhe together to our left on the dance floor.

I can already feel my body wanting to get lost in the loud music as it starts to sway, but we decide to make our way up to the bar first. Turning away from the dance floor, we push our way through the crowd. After a few minutes of waiting, a very hot bartender comes up to us asking us for our drink orders. Ella orders us both vodka sodas.

I sip my drink as I take in the scene around me. Already I feel the tension start to leave my body. "Want to dance," Ella basically yells in my ear over the thumping music.

I nod and we make our way to the dance floor. One Woman Man by John Legend comes on and my body starts to move on its own. I allow all of my problems about Brendan and Kieran to slip away, singing along and letting the music fill my soul. I feel a warm body step up to me, grinding against my back. A hand lands on my hip, but I don't turn around to see who it is because I don't care. My body only wants one man, the one I can't have.

The song changes and I continue dancing with the stranger until I hear a low deep growl right in front of me. The sound causes my whole body to react, the hairs on the back of my neck prickling in anticipation.

Chapter Nine

Brendan

Kieran and I enter the club and head straight to the VIP lounge. Da sent us here to talk to Mikhail, a known billionaire and also the head of the Bratva. We still haven't found out who is stealing from us, but we know that Zeev and Mikhail are missing merchandise too.

We all get drugs, guns, and other items from a few German organizations. My guess is that one of these assholes is taking from us and them too. Now we just have to narrow it down and prove it.

I see Mikhail as soon as we enter the VIP room, standing at the balcony overseeing his kingdom. I notice that his gaze stays focused on someone in particular. Kieran and I make our way toward him. Mikhail's bodyguard notices us first and notifies him. He turns toward us and grins, greeting us, "Boys, so happy to have you here."

His slight accent is the only indication that he's Russian since, like Kieran and I, he grew up in the States. His family came over a few generations ago, taking over the Bratva. Mikhail is about ten years older than me and still loves to party. After indulging in the club scene so much, he decided to open up his own. The media loves to call him the Russian Playboy Prince.

I grin back at him, shaking his hand. "Mikhail, it's been a bit. I love what you've done to the place."

"Yes, this is something," Kieran chimes in as he looks around the room and his eyes hone in on someone across the room.

"I heard that you might have gotten some information that you wanted to share with us."

Mikhail nods his head. "Yes, my sources tell me that one of our allies is double-crossing us. There are whispers that our German allies might have a group of rebels within them."

He just confirmed what I was thinking, but we need more intel. "Do you have any thoughts of who it could be?"

Mikhail seems to give it some thought before he says, "No but I've had some run-ins with a Johann, but that doesn't answer why he would be stealing from Zeev and you."

"Not sure who this Johann could be. I've never heard of him but maybe Da had some run-ins with him..." Before I can finish, my eyes turn to the dance floor and that's when I see her. She looks fucking stunning, freer than she has in ages, dancing away with her friend Ella. It brings a small smile to my face.

As I'm drinking her in, another man saddles up behind her and puts his hand on her hip.

"Motherfucker." Before I even realize what I'm doing, I'm making my way toward her. No one touches what's mine.

I stand in front of her trying to contain the beast within, growling out, "What are you doing, Suri?"

Her body instantly reacts to my voice. That's my girl. Before she can think any better of it, she moves toward me leaving the man who touched her behind. I grab her wrist and pull her into my chest, I lean down and rub my nose against her neck, snuggling into her.

"Fuck, you smell so good."

We start to sway with the music, losing ourselves in one another. This is what I miss. It's been four years and she still lights me up like no other. I grind my cock against her pussy. "Do you feel what you still do to me, princess?"

She lets out a small whimper as I grind even harder into her. My hand comes around her neck bringing the shell of her ear closer to my mouth and I whisper, "You're coming home with me."

"I can't."

"Princess, it's not a choice. You will come home with me."

She wrings her hands together. She's nervous. Her eyes leave mine and gaze behind me. I follow her line of sight to Kieran with another woman. I shake my head. He is an ass to be hitting on someone right in front of her.

But I don't give a shit about what he does and neither should she.

"You don't need to worry about him. You won't be marrying him," I whisper in her ear.

I wrap my arms around her shoulders and yank her toward me so we can leave the club. That's when her ring catches my eye. I slide it off her finger. "You are mine."

I grab her, dragging her toward Kieran. I place the ring in his suit pocket. Tapping it, I meet his eyes. "She doesn't need this anymore."

Kieran chuckles and looks at where our hands are connected. "I can see that."

Turning back toward Suri, I lean down and kiss her before she can refuse me. She needs the reminder that she belongs to me and me alone.

"It's over, Princess. You're mine." She grabs my arm to steady herself. I know she doesn't quite believe it can be true. It all seems unreal to her but I'll spend the rest of my life proving it to her.

"Come on, baby. Let's go home."

"I need to make sure Ella is okay before we leave."

"No, you don't. Ella will be fine."

"Brendan, we came together. I'm not just going to leave my friend here without letting her know."

Knowing that Suri won't be content until she knows Ella is safe, I nod my head. She pulls out her phone typing what I assume is a text to Ella. A few minutes later it lights up and she smiles, letting out a soft giggle "Apparently, Ella is going home with someone too."

Fuck, I love her giggles. I will work for the rest of my life to hear more of them. I grab her hand and lock my fingers with hers, heading for the exit.

When the valet pulls up with the car, I usher Suri inside as quickly as possible. I don't want to give her too much time to rethink going home with me. She is quiet the whole ride to my penthouse. Suri has to work things out on her own. She is very independent, stubborn, selfless, caring and smart. All of these things are what I love about her, but they also piss me off sometimes.

I look over at her and shit, she still takes my breath away. No matter how many times I look at her.

"Suri, you are beautiful."

She looks back at me with a look that I can't quite decipher. I place my hand on her thigh, squeezing it. "Are you okay?"

Nodding her head, she whispers, "I'm just a little nervous."

Pulling into the parking lot, I pull into a spot and turn off the car. Turning toward Suri, I grab her neck pulling her closer to me. Touching our foreheads together, I try to use my words to reassure her. "Don't worry, baby. I will take care of you."

The primal beast within me has been waiting so long for this it howls inside me. I want to claim her. Right here in the car will be just fine. I have to tamp that down though. Because this is Suri. She deserves more than a quick fuck in the car.

I need to get her upstairs...in my bed. I want to take my time with her. Savor, lick, bite and taste every inch of her. With that thought, I get out of the car waiting for her by the hood, praying to God she follows me.

Thank fuck she gets out of the car, following me to the elevator. Once we get inside the penthouse, she lets out a gasp and walks toward the reason I bought this place. She makes her way toward the floor-to-ceiling windows that look out over the whole city. She turns to me and whispers softly, "This is beautiful, Brendan."

I brush my hand over her cheek, wiping away a tear that escaped.

"Don't cry. Please. Your tears kill me."

She looks at me and her look of awe changes to desire. Then the most beautiful words slip from her mouth. "I need you, Brendan."

"Don't worry, Princess, you have me. You'll never be able to get rid of me."

Gliding the straps of her dress down her shoulders, the fabric pools at her feet. I step back taking in this goddess in her black strapless bra and thong. She tries to wrap her arms around her body, to hide herself, but that won't do. "Don't you hide from me, Princess. You're perfect."

My words seem to have injected confidence in her because she stands up straighter. My mouth starts to water. I move right in front of her, dropping down to my knees. I grab the waistband of her thong and drag it down her legs, tapping each one so she steps out of it.

Neither one of us says a word, not wanting to break the spell we both seem to be under. I throw her underwear to the side and take in her glistening pussy.

I lean in rubbing my nose along her folds. Suri lets out a small whimper, looking down at me and placing her hands on my cheeks. "Tell me, Princess, has anyone ever tasted this beautiful pussy?"

She shakes her head, never losing eye contact with me. The love that she holds for me shows all over her face and any lingering feelings of doubt that I might've had before vanish. I could never really deny this beautiful creature anything. I will burn down the world to grant her every wish and desire. My feelings are pure love.

Chapter Ten

Brendan

I need to see all of her. Standing up I reach behind her and unclasp her bra, allowing it to fall to the ground. Her breasts bounce and I can't help but stare.

"You are my goddess, princess."

Her beautiful dark areolas are begging me to take them in my mouth. I lean down and suck one of them into my mouth and feel her nipples hardening against my tongue. I hum against her breast as my hand holds onto her waist.

"Brendan," she gasps out.

I ignore her. I need to feel both of her nipples on my tongue. Coaxing out her nipples even more, I keep going. She lets out a mewl, causing me to grin. I move to the other one, sucking it into my mouth as she shudders. She groans my name, then grabs my hair to get my attention.

"Brendan," she says again.

The sharp pull in my scalp goes straight to my already painfully hard dick. "Yes, princess."

"Brendan, I've never done this before. Any of it."

I knew there was a possibility she was a virgin, but it still causes me to pause. Mine. She will only ever be mine. "Don't worry, princess, I'll take care of you. I can't fucking wait to be your first and your last."

I return to her nipples, kneading one with my hand as I engulf the other with my mouth. Suri's body starts to tremble with need. Fuck, she's so responsive to me. I wonder if I could get her to come just from playing with her nipples. She lets out a moan. Fuck, her noises do something to me. I release her nipple with a pop, "Are you going to be my little slut?"

Her body flushes even more with my words. Oh my, the little princess likes it when I talk dirty. Could she be more perfect? I can't wait any longer. My cock wants to be inside her. I pick her up and carry her to the bedroom. I can't let her first time be any less than perfect.

I lay her down on the king-size bed and crawl back down her body. Grabbing her legs, I spread them wide, lean down, and slide the flat side of my tongue through her folds. Goddamit, she tastes fucking delicious. "Shit, princess, you taste like the perfect whore for me."

As I say the words, her pussy floods my mouth. Fuck yes, I take her clit into my mouth and suck. She screams out, "Oh shit, Brendan!"

I keep sucking until she starts writhing uncontrollably underneath me. She sounds like a fucking symphony. I plunge a finger inside her, stroking that perfect spot and not letting up on her clit.

Every cell in my body wants to take her hard and fast, but I know that this needs to be delicate. I insert a second finger, causing her to gasp louder. I double down on her clit when she grabs my hair holding me in place. "Yes, Yes, Yes! Brendan!" she screams out as her body stiffens and her orgasm bursts from her.

I insert a third finger. "That's right, princess, ride my hand. I need you to be ready to take my cock."

Once her orgasm subsides, I unzip my jeans allowing my cock to spring forward. Suri lets out a whine and her hand wraps around it. I let out a hiss. She snatches her hand back with a look of concern on her face. I grab her hand and put it back on my cock. "Don't worry, my slut. I like the way you touch it. Move your hand up and down."

I put my hand on top of hers and show her how I like to be touched. It isn't long before the telltale tingling starts in my spine. "I want to come inside your pussy as you milk my cock."

Moving back up her body, I notch my tip at her entrance. I look into her eyes, hooded with lust. I can see she wants this as much as I do. Leaning down, I kiss her as I push my cock into her inch by inch.

I feel the ring of resistance and pause. I kiss her forehead, "I'm sorry, baby, but this is going to hurt."

Her eyes soften, placing her hand on my cheek. "It's okay, Brendan, I want this."

Kissing her forehead, I push even further into her. She lets out a whimper. I pause a second. "Damn, Suri, you're so tight."

I can see the tears in her eyes. My other hand comes between us and rubs her clit. "You're doing so good, princess. Look at you taking my cock."

With my words I can feel her body start to relax, she stutters out, "M-move, Brendan. I need you to move."

"Who am I to deny my princess?" I start to move slowly at first, making sure that I rub against her clit with my pelvis every time. Looking straight into her eyes, everything around us falls away and it's just us.

"Please, Brendan..."

Grunts and slapping of skin fill the room. I can tell that she's getting closer as her walls start to clench around my cock. "Fuck, princess, you're strangling my cock like the perfect whore that you are."

"Yes, Brendan. I'm coming."

The walls of her pussy tighten around me and I go over the edge with her. "Fucking shit, princess," I grit out as I come inside her.

Feeling exhausted from holding back, I twist to the side, laying her down on my chest with my softening cock inside her. Once I have her settled on me, I pull the blankets up covering both of us.

I look down and run my fingers down the side of her face.

"I love you, Brendan. That was perfect."

My heart clenches knowing that I need to move faster to stop her marriage. Kissing her forehead, I tell her, "Sleep, princess."

It's as if she needed my permission because before I can even finish, her eyes close. She lets out a soft snore and I smile. Fuck, this woman has always had my heart.

I reluctantly pull out of Suri and head to the bathroom. I see her virgin blood on my cock. Mine. She is mine and I will *never* let her go.

Kieran hasn't had the balls to talk to Da so I'm going to have to do it myself. I don't care about the consequences anymore. I climb back into bed and tug her body closer to me. This is just the beginning. This is all I want every night for the rest of our lives.

Now I just have to make it happen.

Chapter Eleven

Suri

I wake up feeling a sense of tranquility. I stretch my limbs and realize how sore my body feels. Memories of last night flash through my mind and a smile comes to my face before I can even stop it. I look over and see Brendan. He looks so disarming when he is asleep. Young. Calm. It reminds me of the boy that I grew up with.

I reluctantly but quietly pull away so I don't wake him. I head to the bathroom to clean up. I can still feel the stickiness between my legs. I finally had sex. Incredible sex.

Sex with Brendan. It's something I dreamed of when we were teenagers, but never thought it would happen once Mallory got her claws in me. Especially after the engagement with Kieran. I can still remember the look of betrayal on Brendan's face when he found out.

Things were never the same after that. I left for school and he closed himself off to me and the world.

I look down at my hand where my engagement ring used to be. I still can't believe he took it off. I don't feel sad that it's gone even after it being on my finger for the last four years. I just feel relieved. When Brendan pulled it off my hand, he took all my worries with it.

Brendan was so sure last night that the only O'Sullivan man I will marry will be him. I hope he's right. I hope he knows what he's doing. I love his possessiveness. I love the sense of safety he makes me feel. He's the only person who has ever proven that he will protect me. I love him.

I still feel a small inkling of doubt in the back of my head though telling me not to get too comfortable. We can make all the plans in the world, but we can't underestimate Mallory. She will not just sit back and let me be happy, especially if the plan doesn't align with her ambitions.

Brendan doesn't know everything. I need to tell him about the threats. Mallory will follow through on them.

Looking at myself in the mirror, I cringe a bit because man I look like a hot mess. My hair is sticking up all over the place, my lips are red and swollen. I rub my fingertips over my lips, remembering how it felt like I would die if he stopped kissing me.

I turn around and head toward the shower. I'm sure Dad and Mallory know that I didn't come home last night. I need all my strength to back Brendan up with this marriage business.

I jump into the shower, letting the hot water fall over my body and kneading my sore muscles. My mind starts to wander. How can I make sure I keep this feeling of peace and happiness?

Maybe if I talk to Dad I can convince him to drop this ridiculous idea of me marrying Kieran. I have never told him straight up that I didn't want to marry him. If I admit to him that I'm in love with Brendan, he'll let me marry him instead. Right?

I know he's not the ideal son from their perspective. In their words, Brendan is a thug and has no future. I've never understood their hatred toward him. He comes from the same family as Kieran. He's not going to be taking over the O'Sullivan business. Who cares? I don't give a crap about that. Dad shouldn't either. He wants me to be happy right? Could I run away and never see my father again?

The thought of talking to my dad seemed like a good idea at first, but the more I thought about it, the more the nerves started to fester. What if I'm wrong and he won't allow me to marry Brendan? I won't survive losing him a second time.

As my thoughts start to lead down a dark path, a hand wraps around my waist and a warm breath whispers into my ear, "Good morning, Princess."

This man...only he could stop my downward spiral. I spin in his arms and can't help but take in how gorgeous he looks. I'm sure my eyes widened a bit because Brendan is ripped. The man definitely works hard on his body. Towering over me at six foot three with shoulders so wide that they take up most of the shower area. Slowly making my way down, I pause at his muscular pecs, taking them in. All I want to do is rub my hands all over them. Taking him in more, holy crap abs! I didn't even notice last night that he had an eight pack. But now I'm thinking about what it would be like to trace them with my tongue. Licking my lips, I'm drawn to the muscular V that leads to his delicious cock. A cock that is standing straight up, pointing toward me. I rise on my tip toes and give him a chaste kiss. "Good morning."

Starting to pull away so I can finish washing up, his grip tightens. "Where do you think you're going, princess?"

I let out a laugh, trying to push him away playfully "Let me go. I need to wash up."

His voice grumbles into my ear "Why would you wash up when I'm just going to get you dirty again?"

My thighs clench together with the thought of him dirtying me up again. I can feel the heat between my legs.

Brendan leans down and kisses me. He starts off soft, brushing against my lips, opening them with his tongue. But the softness only lasts so long before it's all teeth and tongue and passion.This kiss is full of promises and love. It holds strength and doesn't back down.

As we're kissing he lifts me and my legs instantly wrap around him. I can feel his cock rubbing against my core, making me wetter. I rotate my hips toward him, trying to draw him inside. Brendan denies me and keeps his cock on the outside of my pussy.

He makes a humming sound. "Is my pussy being a greedy girl?"

I don't answer him with words. I couldn't even if I tried. Now that I know what his body feels like, I want it even more. I rotate my hips some more and let out a whimper as soon as I feel the head of his cock against my clit. Brendan still doesn't allow himself inside of me. He tightens his hands on my thighs to stop me from moving.

Becoming desperate, I mutter out "P..p..please, Brendan"

He pulls away from me with a mischievous grin. "Well, since you asked nicely, princess."

Without warning, he thrusts into me all the way to the hilt. I'm so sore but it doesn't matter, my pussy takes him like it was made for him. And I guess in many ways it was, it has never wanted anyone else but Brendan.

I clench around him. "Hell yes! I'm already so close."

Brendan fucks me fiercely and I love it. He thrusts in and out of me against the shower wall. The coolness of the tile and the warmth of his body overwhelm my senses and before I know it, I'm coming. "Brendan!" I scream at the top of my lungs.

He keeps fucking me, losing rhythm as he gets closer to his release. Then I see his abs clench and fuck it's the most beautiful sight I've ever seen. I feel the warmth of his cum filling my body. He stills, leaning impossibly closer to me pressing me into the shower wall. His forehead rests against mine and we breathe together in silence.

"Princess," he says one final time before he kisses me like I'm the most precious thing in the world.

He gently puts me down but his eyes never leave my thighs where his cum slowly slides out of me. I watch as he takes his fingers and wipes up his come and brings it to my mouth. "Be a good little whore and lick up our come."

I take his finger into my mouth and lick. It tastes salty, musky, and a little bit sweet. His eyes flare with excitement as I swallow.

"You are such a good little slut."

We wash up and get out of the shower. I grab a pair of Brendan's shorts and one of his shirts to wear. I can't wear my dress from last night and my underwear is ruined.

As we are finishing up, my phone rings and I see Mallory's name on my screen. Shit, I don't want to deal with this, but if I don't answer, she'll punish me even more.

I take a deep breath, answering in the calmest voice that I can muster, "Yes, Mallory."

"Where the fuck are you, Suri?"

Brendan looks at me with a raised eyebrow and I try to ignore him. My hands start to sweat as I speak as calmly as possible. "I stayed with Ella last night."

She screeches literally like a cat. "Don't give me that shit. I know you didn't stay with Ella. Come home now, Suri. I mean it." Then before I can answer her, she hangs up.

I look up at Brendan. I just shrug my shoulders as he moves close enough to wrap me in his arms.

"I guess it's time."

Chapter Twelve

Brendan

After the phone call Suri received from the witch, I didn't want to take Suri home. I didn't like the way she talked to her. No one should talk to my princess like that. Unfortunately, Suri was her typical, stubborn self and insisted that I take her home and let her deal with Mallory.

Suri has endured Mallory for years, but she's still naive to the power that she holds. Suri only sees what Mallory allows her to see. She doesn't give a crap about anyone unless they can fill up her bank account. The fucking epitome of a gold digger.

The idea of marriage between our families came from Mallory. She gave Richard the seed and helped it grow. When my Da brought up the alliance and mentioned that Mallory was campaigning for it, I had Henry look into her background. He didn't find anything out of the ordinary, but nothing about her seemed right.

My gut tells me that she's dangerous. And now that she has her clutches in Richard, she won't let go and it's obvious she thinks she can use the connection between Suri and Kieran to insert herself into my family. I won't allow it. I will try to ruin her without killing her, I don't want Suri to have to carry any guilt. But if I need to, I won't hesitate. My number one priority is making sure that Suri is free and safe from Mallory.

We pull up in front of Suri's family mansion. Staring out the window, my gut screams at me to turn around and get her out of here. If Suri goes into the house, she might not come out as the same person.

"You know you don't have to do this; I will protect you."

"I need to face them and let them know that I won't be marrying Kieran. Plus Mallory will..."

Suri's eyes get real big and she slams her mouth shut. I narrow my eyes at her. "Mallory will what, Suri?"

"Nothing... just Mallory will be mad. I need to do this myself." Then she pulls her lip into her mouth, biting down on it. I take my finger and rub against it, releasing it from her teeth.

I lay my forehead against hers and whisper, "I can't lose you, Suri. Call me if you need anything. I'm going to talk to Da about the marriage with Kieran."

She nods and kisses me. "I love you, Brendan." With those words, she leaves the car and enters the mansion. And I feel as if my whole heart just left the car with her.

I drive toward my father's estate. Kieran promised he would tell Da to pull the marriage arrangement, but he's an asshole. I'm sure he hasn't done it yet or I would have heard about it. Well, I don't give a shit. I'm tired of waiting. It's time to force him and Da to stop this marriage and take the consequences. I have always lived for the family, but it's time to live for Suri.

Entering the mansion, a sense of calm comes over me. This visit will change everything in my life and even though I should be nervous, I'm not. When this charade ends, I get Suri. No one will come between us, not even my family. I nod to Finn, the man who runs the household for my Da, following him toward the dining room.

Da is sitting at the head of the table reading a newspaper with his breakfast in front of him. Ma is to his left reading the lifestyle section of the paper. No one reads newspapers anymore. I shake my head. My parents are nothing but traditional.

They both look up at the same time. Da has on his mask of indifference. I'm sure he's wondering what I'm up to now. Ma smiles at me. "Brendan! Good morning, son! To what do we owe the pleasure of your visit?"

Ignoring Da until it's time, I smile back at my Ma. The anchor of our family. "Da, Ma, I've come here to talk to you about the marriage between Kieran and Suri."

Both of my parents place their newspapers down and straighten their backs with my words. My Ma looks intrigued, but Da looks downright furious. I place my hands by my side, preparing for a battle if necessary.

Da speaks first. "There's nothing to talk about, it's a done deal. Kieran knows his duty." He tries to wave me off, telling me he doesn't want to discuss it any further.

I look straight at my Da, growling out, "It doesn't matter if Kieran knows his duty. She is mine, not his."

He scoffs at me. "She is not yours. Suri's family has already agreed to the marriage. If you stop this arrangement, then you will bring the word of this family into question. Disgracing our family's name and I will not allow that to happen, Brendan."

I slam my fists down on the table, causing my mother to jump but I don't allow that to deter me. I can't show any weakness with him. I grit out, "I don't care about the family's reputation. I only care about Suri and she will be marrying me."

Out of the corner of my eye, I can see Ma's eyes jumping back and forth between Da and me. I can tell that she wants to say something but she knows better than to interrupt.

Silence encases the dining room as we just stare at each other. Only heaven breathing fills the air. My Da grits his teeth and his right eye twitches, that's how I know that he's fucking pissed. But I don't give a shit. I've been pissed at him about this nonsense for the last four years.

"Fine, I will end the arrangement between Suri and Kieran, but you will pay the consequences."

Before even stepping into the mansion, I knew my Da would make me pay. He always makes us pay for our actions. I don't know what the price will be, but I'll pay anything. I take a deep breath, nodding. "Spit it out, Da."

"You will be in exile, Brendan. I want you to think really hard about this. You are forbidden to have any contact with anyone associated with this family."

My Ma's face falls with my Da's words. I nod my head, indicating that I understand. I start to turn and leave with my head held high when I hear Ma's soft voice, "Brendan."

I turn around and can see the anguish on her face. She walks toward me, grabs my cheeks, pulls me closer, and whispers, "Is she worth it?"

"Ma, she is worth everything. I've been in love with her since the day I met her."

I can see a sense of peace come over her as she pulls me down and kisses my forehead. "I love you, son."

I leave the family mansion ready to go get my princess.

Chapter Thirteen

Suri

Even though I tried to be strong in front of Brendan, I could feel my anxiety starting to spread through my body. In my head I practiced my anxiety exercises while he drove me home. I didn't want him to see how much uncertainty I was feeling. He wouldn't have dropped me off at home and I need to do this. It's time I stand up for myself. I can't let my dad and Mallory rule my life forever.

I think back to the night before the gala when she brought up the marriage contract. Honestly, I thought it was a joke. I laughed and told both of them that I was too young to get married. Let alone to Kieran. I didn't even really know him. Why would I want to marry someone I didn't even know?

After dinner, my dad called me to his office and sat me down. I can still feel the brick that started to grow in my stomach that night. They were serious. "Mallory and I have been talking and we feel that you marrying Kieran will help strengthen our family and its power. Kieran is the firstborn son and will be a true leader one day. I won't force you, but I need you to think about the responsibility you have to this family and what it could mean to us."

Leaving Dad's office that night, I went up to my room where Mallory cornered me, threatening my safety and my dad's to make sure I complied. She even sent me reminders over the last four years to make sure she kept me under her thumb.

But what she didn't know was that her threats only gave me strength. Forging me into someone stronger who knows her worth. Now it's time to stand up for myself and put Mallory in her place. She doesn't know that I've been gathering information on her. I don't like confrontation, but the one thing Mallory did was teach me to protect myself. And that's exactly what I'm going to do.

Before last night, I never thought Brendan would want to marry me, so I didn't see the need to end the charade. Now that he has claimed me, it's time to stop this mess.

I have plans for the future. It's time to start living for myself.

Standing in front of the door, my confidence starts to wane a bit. I mutter under my breath, "You got this, Suri."

I straighten my shoulders, take one last breath and enter the mansion.

I walk into the living room to find my Dad and Mallory sitting on the couch whispering to each other. They both seem tense, but Mallory is giving off waves of anger. Something is going on, but that doesn't matter. It's showtime.

"Dad, can I talk to you?"

My dad looks over to me with concern written all over his face. He looks me over, furrowing his brows when he takes in my attire and then rumbles out. "Suri, where have you been? We've been worried about you!"

"I'm sorry, Dad. I didn't mean to worry you. I went out last night with Ella."

Which is true, but not the whole truth. If he knew what I did last night, it would be even more awkward.

"We know that you weren't with Ella," Mallory rudely interrupts.

Usually, I would cower if she talked to me that way but not today. I'm going to show her exactly who I've become. I look straight into her eyes before I state matter of factly, "I was with Ella last night. We went to the new club, Midnight."

As we continue to stare at each other, never breaking eye contact, I feel the tension filling the room. My dad clears his throat and drops the next bit of information "Suri, one of our associates saw you at Brendan's penthouse last night."

Crap, I guess I have to confess more than I wanted to. Mallory interrupts him again and starts to ramble on getting louder and louder as she goes. "Yes, we have proof. You know you're supposed to stay away from him. You're engaged to Kieran. Do you know how this looks? What if he saw you or heard about this? It's his brother, Suri."

Tired of hearing her, I turn my back to her and bring all of my attention to my Dad. "Dad, that's actually what I came to talk to you about. I was with Brendan last night because I love him. I don't want to marry Kieran."

"Suri, we have already committed to this marriage."

I huff trying not to let my anger cloud my thoughts. In a sharper tone than before, I respond, "Dad, you said that you wouldn't force me. I've been in love with Brendan my whole life, which you would know if you ever listened to me before."

My dad grabs my hand and pulls me to sit down next to him on the couch. With a soft voice, he says, "You know, Suri, when you were born I fell in love with you and vowed to give you the best I could. I know I haven't always been there for you...especially after your mom died. If you don't want to marry Kieran and want to be with Brendan. I will support you-"

"Richard. You can't," Mallory interrupts. He gives her that look and she shuts up immediately but I can tell that she's still angry. He stands up. "Let me call Brian and see what we can work out."

With those parting words, he walks to the back of the house toward his office. I wasn't expecting that. I can't believe he gave in so quickly. I thought he would threaten, guilt me, try to make me see the error of my ways. Maybe my dad loves me more than I thought? Happy tears start to well up in my eyes, thinking about how close I am to my happy ending. I can see the light at the end of the tunnel.

I look over at Mallory, and if looks could kill I would be dead right now. I need to get away from her. Besides, I can't wait to call Brendan. As I walk past her, she grabs my arm, her nails digging into my skin.

"You little bitch. You might think you've gotten your way but I will get the last word." Venom drips from her words as she stares at me.

I lean into her and calmly whisper, "You might want to be careful, Mallory, before you push me too far. I won't be marrying Kieran, but I will always be a part of their family."

I can see the disbelief in her eyes. Good. Now she knows what it's like to be threatened. Ripping my arm from her, I walk up the stairs to my bedroom with a smirk on my lips. Closing the door, I grab my phone and dial Brendan.

"Princess." God...that voice does things to me. Just hearing it settles my nerves and makes my thighs clench.

"I talked to my dad and told him I won't marry Kieran. That I love you."

"How did he take it?"

"He said he just wanted me to be happy. Can you believe it? Did you talk to your parents?"

"I did. I have a few things to take care of and we'll talk about it tomorrow. But don't worry. You. Are. Mine."

A huge smile takes over my face. I can't believe things are starting to fall into place. I whisper, "I love you."

"I love you too, princess."

I let out a small gasp, "Brendan, that's the first time you've said that to me."

A sob bursts out of me.

"Princess, why are you crying?"

Sobbing, "N..n...no one has...e..ever told me that they...l... love me before."

"Oh Suri...I will tell you everyday for the rest of our lives. You'll never go without again."

With his words, I smile through the tears. "Brendan." I sigh.

"Go get some rest. We'll meet at the penthouse tomorrow."

"Ok. I'll see you tomorrow,"

I hang up the phone and head toward my computer. Then I do something I haven't done in a while. I write. I work on my book and the words come easier than ever before.

Chapter Fourteen

Suri

I wake up feeling lighter than ever. No more unhappiness. No more uncertainty. No more Kieran. Honestly even a run in with Mallory couldn't bring me down right now. I need to see and feel Brendan as soon as possible. I check my phone and I can't help but smile.

> **Brendan:** Good Morning Princess.

As I read it, I can hear his voice as clear as if he was standing right next to me. I know I have the cheesiest grin on my face. Can this really be happening?

> **Me:** Good Morning! I need to see you. Meet you at the penthouse in an hour?

His response comes back immediately. Seriously...the butterflies. I haven't felt like this in a long time. I never thought about being with anyone but Brendan and then suddenly I was eighteen and engaged to a virtual stranger. I used being engaged as an excuse to keep people away. I encased myself in a life of loneliness. All by my own doing.

Brendan: See you then Princess.

Putting my phone down, I jump up, moving into the bathroom to get ready for the day and going over everything I need to do. First and foremost talk to Brendan and figure out where we go from here. Do we just jump into the deep end or should we take it slow? At this point I don't care. I just want to be with him.

I want to get out from underneath Mallory and my dad. I want to find myself a new apartment. Maybe Ella will go with me to look or she could room with me. Finishing up, I look in the mirror and love what I see. It's been a long time since I felt so good and I think it shows.

Grabbing my purse and my phone, I text Ella. I wonder how everything went with her after I left the club last night.

Me: Hey sorry to leave you last night, but I have so much to tell you. Do you want to have coffee later?

Ella: No worries. I ended up having a great night. Yes, let's do coffee.

Today is going to be the best day ever. I'm going to see Brendan and then have a coffee date with Ella. No one is downstairs as I make my way to the front door. That's weird. Even the staff seems to have disappeared. Usually at least Ariana is around making sure we don't need anything. Not putting too much thought into it, I shrug. Mallory or Dad must have them busy.

I head out the door and notify the driver that I'm ready to leave. Climbing into the car, I lean back against the seat. "Take me to Brendan's penthouse, please."

I don't bother with saying the address. Everyone who works for my dad knows where he lives. He all but admitted last night that those around me report my whereabouts to him.

I put my headphones in turn on my mood booster playlist from Spotify and space out. I never thought the future could look and feel so bright.

A building I don't recognize catches my attention. Crap, why are we heading away from Brendan's penthouse. I pull my headphones out. "Hey, where are we going? You're going the wrong way, let me get you the address."

The driver ignores me. Wait... he looks familiar but I don't remember if he works for my dad or if I know him from somewhere else. My hackles go up and I wrack my brain trying to place the man behind the driver's seat.

I lean forward and tap his shoulder but he abruptly pushes me back. My back slams against the back of the seat. Damn that hurt. As I look up to ask the driver what the hell is going on, I see the divider going up.

Shit, what's happening? This has to be bad, right? I need to call Brendan and get help. I grab my cell phone. Hearing the phone ring helps with my anxiety a bit, but I need to hear his voice.

"Suri, you're late."

Before I can answer him, I hear a loud screech and I jolt forward really hard. "Brendan," I scream.

Then the car jolts again and starts to roll. I'm upside down and all I can hear is Brendan's voice screaming, "Suri!"

I try hard to answer, but I can't. I can't even scream, but my brain is telling me that I need to get out of here. I'm in danger. Coming to my senses I feel something drip down my face. I put my hand up to my head. Pulling it back, I just see red all over my fingers. Crap, is that my blood?

I need to get out of here, I try to move, but I'm still buckled. I eject the seatbelt and fall to the ground...or maybe the roof? Shit, we're upside down. Luckily I was able to put my hands down to brace myself. Glancing around, I see that one of the windows must have broken when we rolled.

Crawling out the window, I ignore the glass embedding itself into my arms and legs. I can deal with the pain later. Right now I need to get out of here. When I'm outside the car, I try to stand up and a wave of dizziness comes over me. Goddammit...think Suri. Think.

Before I can fully stand up I feel something prick the back of my neck. Hell, what was that? I'm so tired. My eyes feel so heavy. No matter what I do I can't keep them open. I need to get to my phone...to call...Brendan...he'll...

In the distance, I think I hear whispers. "We need to get out of here before someone reports us to the police."

"You should call her, Johann."

I try to lift my head. Tell them to call Brendan...then the whole world goes black.

Chapter Fifteen

Suri

Damn, why does my head hurt? I just want to make the pain go away. I try lifting my hands from my side to cradle my head, but I can't. Why can't I move my hands? I panic. I tug and pull but nothing works. Slowly peeling my eyes open feels like it takes a Herculean effort. My eyelids feel glued to the tops of my eyeballs. Glancing down, I notice that I'm sitting in a chair and my hands are tied behind my back. No wonder I couldn't move my hands. I try to move my legs, but when I look down they are also tied to the chair too. Damn, that's not good.

My surroundings are hard to see since I'm enveloped in darkness. As my eyes start to slowly adjust...

"Where the hell am I?" I rasp out. My voice does not even sound like my own. The crash. Little snippets of heading to Brendan's, the driver, glass breaking, hitting my head, and the car rolling flutter through my mind.

My brain flutters with so many thoughts. They feel like they're coming at the same time but one sticks out the most. Johann. Who is Johann?

Suri, look around to see if you can figure out where you are.

Listening to the little voice inside my head, I look around to see if I can identify anything specific. I need to make sure I pay attention to my surroundings, that way if I get away I can let someone know where I am. Dad pounded into me what to do if I ever got kidnapped. He was always so worried that one of his clients would get mad at him and do something foolish. I always thought he was full of it, but here I am.

I think I'm in a warehouse. Maybe one of my dad's? But the more I look, the more I know that I've never been here before.

I try to lean a little farther to the left to see more of the room. My chair rocks a bit and that small movement causes me to wince. My whole body hurts so bad.

Right on cue, more memories of the accident come rushing to the forefront of my mind. I can see myself crawling through the window to get out of the car. That's probably why my legs look cut up. I remember trying to stand up and then feeling dizzy while looking around for my phone. People were talking.

Crap, was someone with me? It was the driver. Did he make it? Did someone hit us?

Then I remember that the driver wasn't even going toward Brendan's house like he was supposed to. Damn, that probably means the driver was in on it. Fear starts to creep up my back as a small tear escapes. *Why is this happening to me?*

Soft footsteps interrupt my thoughts of despair. A tall figure walks toward me. A tall, lean blonde man. I can't seem to place him anywhere. He sneers down at me. "You're awake, Princess."

My skin crawls as if I have ants underneath it. I don't like the way this man calls me princess. That name is only for Brendan. Another wave of sadness hits me, thinking about how crazy Brendan must be going not knowing where I am.

"I can't wait to see what she says when she sees you," the man says, bringing my thoughts back to him. Wait...she? Who's she?

He doesn't say anything else. Just takes me in, turns, and leaves through the same door that he came in.

I can't help but wonder who...No, she wouldn't do this, would she? My dad wouldn't stand for this, so if it's Mallory, she must be doing this behind his back. I shake my head. This seems to be too much.

Think. I need to get out of here before whoever "she" is shows up. Maybe if I just cooperate, I can get them to think that I won't cause any harm and I can convince them to untie my hands. Plans start to go through my head.

The door creaks open and that's when I hear the familiar click of high heels on the concrete. I snap my head up and look toward the noise. Mallory. Damn, I can't believe she did this. She stands there, staring at me as if she's trying to figure out what to do next.

"You know you won't get away with this," I whisper to her. I want her to know that she won't survive this no matter what happens to me.

She just smiles at me and crap if that isn't the scariest thing I've ever seen. She draws her finger down my face, "Oh, Suri. It doesn't matter what happens to me. You won't be making it out of here and that's payment enough. You never should have defied me."

"What about my dad?" I ask with a voice that's stronger than I feel at the moment.

"Richard? He was a pawn from the beginning. I've been playing the long game. You see, Suri, I'm a member of a group of people who are tired of the O'Sullivans and how they rule everything. I couldn't get to them through *their* organization but I could use their allies against them. That's where you and your dad come in. It was so easy. Your dad needed someone to be his partner. I gained his trust over the years, convincing him that I loved him. He never expected the person he married to betray him. Such arrogance. When I brought the idea of your marriage to him, he jumped on it so quickly. But you had to ruin it, didn't you? Don't worry though, I will fix everything. I can bring the O'Sullivans to their knees through you. Granted it might not be the way I thought, but this might be even better."

I just stare at her as she talks. I can't believe she used my dad like this. Tears slide down my cheeks. Mallory grabs my face. "Don't worry, little Suri, you don't need to cry. It will be all over soon."

Despite what Mallory thinks, I'm not crying for myself. I'm crying for how devastated my dad will be when he finds out. The witch is showing her real colors now. The rest of my tears are for Brendan, the man I love. We won't get to have our life together. It's over before it ever started. He must be going insane trying to find me.

Done talking, she pushes me almost causing my chair to fall backwards. She looks at me with nothing but disgust. "Goodbye, Suri. If you were a good girl, maybe this could've ended differently. Maybe we could have been allies. But you let puppy love ruin everything. I'll get Brendan too, don't worry."

"You leave him alone, you bitch!" I scream as she closes the door.

Chapter Sixteen

Brendan

"Suri!" I scream into the phone.

This can't be happening. I wince as I hear her breathing into the phone, but she doesn't make a sound. The sound of metal crunching and then the glass breaking comes through the phone and I know what is going on, she has been hit. My heart is beating faster and faster. I smash my hands to my head. Think Brendan...think.

I pull my phone out and call Henry. "She's hurt," I rush out as soon as he picks up.

"Brendan, what do you mean?"

"Suri, I was on the phone with her. Then I heard her screaming and the car crashing."

"Man, you need to calm down. Did you check her location?"

I switch to the tracking app and check her location. The dot shows that she is out in the middle of nowhere, nowhere close to the penthouse. "Fuck, why is she out there?"

"Brendan, where is she?"

"I'll send you her location. Meet me there."

Grabbing my keys off of the counter, I head toward the elevator. When the doors open, I go straight to my car. I drive like a madman to her last location.

"Get the fuck out of my way!" Goddammit, I'm yelling at every car on the road. If I don't get pulled over, it will be a miracle. Do I care about a ticket...fuck no! I heard her scream my name. I heard the glass and the crunching of the metal.

What the fuck happened? I need to get to her and make sure she's okay. I keep checking the dot on her phone. I see her location, she's not moving. I'm only five minutes out and it's feeling like fucking five hours.

She's okay. She has to be okay.

Approaching her location, I slam on brakes and skid to a stop. Flying out of the car, I scream at the top of my lungs, "Suri!"

Henry pulls up shortly after me. When he flings himself from the car, he rushes straight for me. "Brendan, why did I just fucking get a call saying that you were exiled?"

I turn towards him, answering him with one word, "Suri,"

With a look of understanding, he turns and moves toward the wreckage.

I'm lucky to have Henry in my life. Someone so loyal that even my exile doesn't stop him from helping. A real brother.

We both stand there taking in the scene. Henry speaks first.

"Fuck, what the hell happen?"

The car is smashed in and rolled over on the side of the highway. Glass everywhere.

I don't answer him. I look in the car, shouting, "Suri. Come on, baby, talk to me, tell me where you are?"

Something deep in my gut tells me she's not here. I glance down and I see blood. My first thought is NO!

Walking around the car, I take in the scene and check again that she didn't get thrown. I find her phone laying on the ground. "Fuuuck."

My fists clench. We didn't find her body. I can feel it deep in my bones that someone took her. A haze of red starts to tint my eyes.

I have to get her back, in one piece, alive. If someone touched her...they will burn. She's bleeding...

Through the fog, I hear a faint voice calling my name. Still clenching my fists I try to maintain a clear head, but it's hard. She's bleeding...I hear the voice again calling my name. This time I feel hands on my shoulders, shaking me. The haze over my eyes clears a bit and I can see Henry standing in front of me looking a bit concerned. "Fuck, Brendan. Come on man. Keep it together."

She's not here. Where could she be? "They took her."

His face softens a little which pisses me off even more. I don't need pity, I need him to help me find her. I have to keep a clear head so I ask him, "What did you find?"

"I didn't find her but they did leave someone behind."

"Someone?"

"Yeah, I found a body hidden in the bushes. I'm guessing the driver. He's over here."

I follow Henry to where he found the body. I don't recognize him but assume he is one of the drivers from her mansion. Why else would Suri get in the car with him? I squat down to check his pockets. Pulling out his phone, I check the last person he called.

"Henry, do you recognize the name Johann?"

He shakes his head. "No, I can't think of anybody with that name. But I also can't help shake the feeling that the name is familiar."

I feel the same way. Then it comes to me. Mikhail mentioned Johann, a German associate. And it's the only clue we currently have to find Suri.

Henry and I look around some more to make sure that we didn't miss anything before we head back.

Before we part ways, I ask Henry, "Call Mikhail and see if you can find more about this Johann? Other than that he is a German associate. I want to know everything about him."

He nods his head then places his hand on my shoulder, "Yeah, man. But you need to call Kieran."

I wince at his suggestion, "I know."

I start the car and head back to the penthouse, Henry's suggestion running through my mind.

Grabbing my phone, I hover over his number not sure if he will even talk to me. Will he be willing to help me? Fuck it, I need to do it. I hit the call button.

"Brendan?"

When he answers, I feel a rush of relief. He's still my brother even after Da banished me. We were close as kids until Da thought he should be engaged to Suri. I felt betrayal from everyone and distancing myself was the only way I could survive.

"Kieran. I need your help."

He lets out a small sigh, already frustrated with me. "Brendan, you know I can't. Da's exiled you."

"Suri is missing."

"What do you mean Suri is missing?"

I bristle a little when I hear a growl of possession in his voice. This is not the time to get in a pissing contest with him. I need to find her and if he can help me do it, I'll put up with mountains of shit. I just need her alive.

"You heard me, she's missing. She called me from the car on the way to the penthouse. I didn't get any info before I heard the car crash. I've been to the site...rolled car, only the driver was left behind. It's suspicious as hell..obviously."

"I can't help you. Da will kill me. Have you called Henry?" Kieran replies with a hint of distress. Da and Kieran can't look weak, and by now, word of my decision would have spread.

"Yeah, Henry knows."

"I'll call Henry and give him permission to help you. And let Da know too."

Not needing anything else, I hang up the phone. I'm grateful that Kieran didn't turn me away.

The next call I have to make will be even harder than calling Kieran. Suri's dad answers the phone, "Brendan? Why are you calling me? Is everything okay with Suri?"

Taking a deep breath, I tell him. "Sir, I hate to say this, but Suri is missing. Henry and I are looking for her. We will keep you updated."

Chapter Seventeen

Suri

I'm in a darn nightmare. I'm filthy. Crusted blood covers my face and hands. My body hurts and I'm tired. So, so tired. The only time I'm allowed to move is to use the bathroom and eat two times a day. If I'm not doing one of those things then they have me strapped in a chair with my arms tied behind me. Like what am I going to do? A huge German dude who is like three times my size, watches me all the time. I could never overpower him, but I guess they aren't taking any chances.

"It's been five days, princess. Where is your prince now?"

"He must be more of a frog because he can't even save his princess."

I just roll my eyes. Not giving them the luxury of seeing me upset which upsets him more. I get the impression that he's hoping to make me cry, but I lived the last four years locked up in some way. I won't show him my tears.

Getting through this and seeing my dad and Brendan is the only thing keeping me going. I can't see my way out. I imagine myself dying in this room, dirty and alone.

Five days? How many more can I make? Staring ahead, I mutter with no emotion, "He's coming and you should be scared."

Of course the jerk laughs in my face, not thinking that Brendan is anything to be worried about. I really hate him. If I could move my arms, I would punch him in his ugly face. But my arms hurt. My shoulders burn. And my wrists feel like they're on fire where the ties bind them.

My eyes sting with tears, but I push them back. I will not let them fall. Clicking heels distract me from my thoughts. I know exactly who's coming. Man, I wish she would just stay away. I really don't want to see her.

Lifting my head as she comes closer, our eyes connect. I refuse to cower. She approaches staying silent for a moment. I'm not sure what she's waiting on since she obviously came here for a reason.

"You don't have anything to say?" she asks.

I don't respond.

A smile suddenly starts to creep over her face. A scary, maniacal kind of smile. "Good news. Well for me, maybe not you. The O'Sullivan's are working overtime to try to find you. Which means some of my guys on the inside have been able to steal inventory from them. Your dad even mentioned that they are going to start pulling their other resources together, which also means my spies in those organizations can take from them too."

Not even sure how to react, I just stare ahead. I don't say anything. She wants to break me through Brendan and my dad and she wants to destroy them by killing me. I will not allow it to happen. She turns toward my guard to give him instructions, and that's when I whisper, "Why do you hate me?"

Mallory slowly turns her body with a quizzical look.

"I don't hate you. You are just the means to get what I need, but I can't deny that it does make me happy to see you brought down a peg. The beautiful princess, ugly and lost, never to get her prince."

As I'm starting to feel sorry for myself, I'm jerked up. I let out a yelp with the sudden sharp pain to my shoulder. He's pulling it out of the socket. "Stop! That hurts!"

He just ignores me and leads me to an approaching black SUV similar to the one I crashed in. Crap, he's going to throw me in the backseat.

And just like predicted, he pulls open the back door and I'm thrust into the back seat. "Hell that hurts!" I yell.

I can't help it, I'm in pain. I roll onto my side as the car jerks forward. After we've been driving for what feels like an hour, I'm able to roll into a more comfortable position. But with my hands tied behind my back, I'm still in a lot of pain. I have to adjust constantly to take pressure off my body. I know I need to rest but I can't. After what feels like a few hours, the car slams on the breaks. My eyes pop open and then the car jerks to the side again. Hell, this is another car accident?

I try to brace myself, but that's easier said than done. Rolling up into a fetal position seems to be the only way that I can stop myself from flying everywhere. The car swerves all around, trying to avoid whatever seems to be in the way. Then I hear gun fire. The car seems to jump and then lean to the side. A scream is torn from me as the whole car flips over. I'm tossed all over, slamming my body against god knows what. When I finally stop moving, my head seems to be swimming and I feel like I'm floating. Blackness surrounds me, except for a small bit of light. I try to float toward it but I can't quite get there. That's when I hear it.

"Suri."

Is someone calling my name? It sounds so familiar. Am I imagining it?

"Suri," I hear again, but it seems so far away. I pause waiting to see if I hear it again. Nothing. I must've been imagining it. Trying to get my body to float back toward the light, I hear it again.

"Suri." This time it's closer. I whisper, "Brendan?"

When no one responds, I try again. "Brendan."

"Suri, baby, where are you?" I hear him again. I don't know how to tell him where I am. I just seem to be floating in a vast nothingness, so I just start yelling for him. "Brendan!"

The blackness surrounding me seems to be fading away into what looks like the sky. I hear him yelling for me again, "Suri!"

I need to get to him. I scream his name as loud as I can. "Brendan!" All of a sudden, I see the most beautiful face I've ever seen. It's him! He found me.

Brendan rubs my face as he whispers, "It's ok, princess. I'm here."

"It hurts. Everything hurts. I can't get to the light," I whisper. I close my eyes, then I remember I need to tell him.

"Stay with me, Princess. You're ok. Suri...Suri?"

Then everything goes black again.

Chapter Eighteen

Brendan

T hank fuck she's alive. I keep those words running through my head as I lean down and rub the back of my hand against her cheek.

Suddenly the calm I thought I was able to grasp flies out the window as Suri faints in my arms. Shit, this cannot be happening.

"Suri! Wake up," I tell her as I hug her to me making sure that I can feel her chest move with every breath.

Henry hears me and his footsteps pound to the ground as he rushes over. "Is she hurt? The ambulance should be here in a few minutes."

I don't say anything. I can't. All my words and thoughts are stuck in my chest. The only thing I can do is hold her, whispering in her ear, "Come back to me, Princess."

The sound of sirens gets closer. Before I can react, two men lean down trying to get to Suri. I grip her tighter pulling her closer to my chest. I can't let her go.

"Sir, we need to take her to make sure she's okay." Shaking my head, I bear my teeth at them. I won't allow them to take her from me. She. Is. Mine.

Feeling a hand on my shoulder, I hear Henry say, "You gotta let her go, man. She needs to be checked. They'll take good care of her."

I know he's right but it's so hard. They put a brace around her neck and start to shuffle her onto the backboard to load her up into the ambulance. I can't make my body move. I just stare as they take my world away from me.

The EMT's heading to the ambulance snaps me out of my daze. Determined to be with her, I start to climb in with Suri. The same man who tried to take her from me stops me, "Sir, we can't let you ride with her. It's family only."

Hell, what is this crap? "I'm her goddamned fucking husband so get the fuck out of my way."

He gulps but doesn't say anything else as we stare at each other, neither of us making a move. The other EMT drops his arms and gruffly says, "Don't be an ass, Steve, he can ride with her."

With those words, I don't waste any more time and finish climbing into the ambulance. I grab her hand. She feels so small and fragile. From somewhere in the distance, I hear Henry yell that he'll meet me at the hospital.

The ride to the hospital is fast and slow at the same time. I whisper to her the entire way and growl at the fucking EMTs who I'm afraid are hurting her. She never wakes up, never opens her eyes. I'm losing my goddamn mind. Arriving at the hospital the EMTs rush Suri inside. I try to follow her but a hand settles firmly on my chest. I look up and see a tiny blonde woman looking at me. She looks at me softly, but her words leave no room for argument. She sounds like Ma. "Sir, I know you're worried but you can't follow. We need to let the doctors check her out."

I know she's right, but I feel like I can barely breathe the further she gets from me. I just stare at her. Words run through my mind, but none of them leave my lips. It's like my whole body is wrapped in a fog of uncertainty. Suri has been missing for five days and now she's hurt.

Why did I waste so much time staying away from her? I should have accepted the consequences of being exiled a long time ago. I should have followed her to school and told her I loved her. My whole body shakes.

"Sir, take a breath. I promise you I will let you know something as soon as I can," the nurse tells me. "Breathe," she says again.

Henry walks up next to me. His eyes bounce back and forth between me and the nurse, probably trying to figure out how much damage I've created in the few moments since I arrived. He finally breaks the silence, "What's going on here?"

She sighs and then looks over at Henry. "I was just informing your friend here that he has to stay in the waiting room while the doctors check on the young lady that he came in with."

Henry nods his head in understanding. "Don't worry, we'll wait here for the doctors."

She nods, but before she can walk away I need to make sure she knows to come talk to me right away. "I want the doctor to talk to me as soon as he knows anything."

The nurse's eyes crinkle at the edges a bit and she sets her hand on my arm. "I will make sure they know." With those words, she walks away hopefully to check on Suri.

Dropping my body down in a chair in the waiting room, I lean forward with my elbows on my knees and my head in my hands. Fuck, she has to be okay. I grab my phone to call her dad and let him know that I found her, trying to give myself something to do.

He answers on the first ring, "Brendan?"

"Richard. We found Suri, we have her at the hospital. I'll have her call you as soon as the doctors come out."

Richard sighs, I can feel the relief from him through the phone. "Thank you, Brendan. Thank you for saving my daughter. I'm leaving now. I'll be there soon."

Grunting, I hang up the phone, not able to say anything else. I'm already teetering on the edge. I need to maintain as clear of a head as possible.

Neither Henry nor I say anything to each other. We just sit...waiting. After about an hour, I can't take it any longer. I get up and start to pace back and forth in the waiting room.

Henry just looks up at me, but he doesn't reprimand me. He knows I can't sit still on a good day, let alone in this shitstorm. After what feels like days, the doctor comes out and walks right toward us. "Are you here with Suri?"

"Yes. How is she?"

Wait, did he just say Suri? I never told him her name. That has to be good news right? She must-

The doctor interrupts the questions that are popping up in my head. "She's doing better. She's very bruised. She has a dislocated shoulder and a few cracked ribs plus a concussion. She will need lots of rest over the next few days. She is awake and asking for you, would you like to come with me to see her?"

I don't even have to answer, I just follow the doctor back to her room. Standing at the doorway, with her laying in the hospital bed with her eyes closed, I almost break. She looks so small and she has bandages all over her and an IV in her hand. I can see all the bruises I had missed when I'd first laid eyes on her. I close my eyes and take a deep breath. I have to take care of her now. The anger has to be set aside for later.

She must sense me because before I can even make a move toward her, her eyes pop open. A small smile graces her lips. I make my way toward her, and whisper, "Hey, Princess."

As soon as the words come out of my mouth, she breaks out into a sob. I move quicker to get as close to her as I can without hurting her. Pushing her curls out of her face, I just talk. "Don't worry, princess, everything is going to be fine now. I won't let anything else happen to you. Don't cry. I'm here. I love you. I've always loved you. I'm never leaving you again."

Hiccups well up out of her crying. She might be the fucking cutest thing I have ever seen, bruises and all.

My heart swells as I stare at her. Fuck, she is the most beautiful woman in the world and I love to call her princess, but she is definitely my queen.

Taking my thumb, I wipe away the tears falling down her cheeks. She mutters something, but I can't tell what she said. I kiss her forehead. "It's ok, Suri. Calm down, Princess. Then you can tell me what you want to say."

Suri hears my words and tries to take a deep breath. I watch her close her eyes. With her eyes closed I can tell that she is counting and her chest starts to rise and fall slower and slower. She opens her eyes. "Brendan, I have something to tell you."

I nod at her, grabbing her hand. I squeeze it hoping it's comforting her. "Tell me, Suri."

"Mall...Mallory was the one who took me."

My eyes go wide and I get up, starting to pace. Grabbing my phone, I go to call Henry, but then she says something that makes me stop dead in my tracks. "She's stealing from your dad and whoever else he works with."

I turn to look at Suri. "Are you sure? What exactly did she say?"

"She told me that she's been using me and my dad to get into your dad's organization. That since they've been distracted looking for me, they started to take stuff from you. And they were going to start doing the same to his associates."

Nodding, remembering back to the day after the dinner we had at Suri's house. My Da and Zeev discussed that both of them had inventory go missing. Both of them were worried and had sent me to Mikhail for intel. He was the one who gave me the tip that it was someone from the Germans.

Starting to put the pieces together, I ask her one last question. "Do you remember anything about the people who were with you while you were missing?"

She nods then whispers, "There were really only a few that I saw, but they were tall and had German accents."

I knew it, Mikahil was right! She then adds, "One of the guys' names was Johann."

Of course, the driver was connected to Mallory. I look at my beautiful Suri, knowing I need to make one last phone call before all of this can end. My Da needs to know about this. I owe him and Kieran this piece of information since they were willing to help me. Da gruffly answers, "Brendan. Did you find Suri?"

"I did Da, but that's not why I'm calling." I take a deep breath, knowing this was going to piss Da off. "Suri told me something interesting when she woke up at the hospital."

"Well, tell me, boy."

Trying not to bristle with his tone, I start, "Mallory is the one who took her and she's also the one who's been taking merchandise from you and your allies. She's been playing the long game and taking advantage of Richard and his connections. Suri also said there was a guy named Johann and we found evidence of him being involved in the kidnapping too."

Da is silent for a beat. "Thanks, Bren. I will pass this onto Kieran, but you know you can't be involved right? You're still exiled. The only thing you can do is take care of Suri. I will take care of this."

I grit my teeth. I don't like the idea of my Da taking over but I know in this situation his business takes priority. Staring at Suri, I accept my fate right then and there, whispering, "Okay, Da."

With those last words, I hang up. Suri is my destiny and it's time I take a hold of it. Needing to feel her in my arms, I sit on the bed and hold her. "I love you, Suri."

She lets out a soft sigh, "I love you too, Brendan."

Chapter Nineteen

Suri

It's been weeks since the kidnapping and Brendan still won't let me out of his sight. He let up a little once his dad found Mallory and her accomplice Johann. Brian handed them back over to the New Social movement, who are rumored to actually be the German Mafia. Both of them were suspected to be members of a small rebel group called the NSU-Kemetery, marking them as traitors. Wanting to gain more power to 'supposedly' take over.

All I really care about is that Brendan isn't involved anymore. Telling his Da that he was going to marry me went against his wishes, causing his dad to exile him from the business and from the family. His Ma still talks to him a little even though she's not supposed to, but his Da refuses, and even though he doesn't say it, I know that hurts him.

I look around my room as I pack up my things. It's such a bitter-sweet feeling. On one hand, besides my time in college, this is the only house I've ever lived in. But this house does have memories attached to it that are hurtful too. I can still hear Mallory berating me and feel her striking me in every room I walk into.

The last few weeks have been filled with Brendan and me talking about what we want the future to look like. Including my whispered confessions about wanting to become a published writer. As always he gave me that sexy grin and confidently said, "You'll do it."

That night Brendan gave me a confession of his own. Apparently a man named Zeev that his Da worked with gave him a card from a security firm. Brendan called them and the owner Jake offered him a job, but it's located in Los Angeles. Smiling up at him, "'Let's do it. A new start."

Honestly the move allows me to breathe a little bit more. It's far away from everything we know, but we want to move forward and not look back. My phone dings with a text. I glance down at Ella's name and a huge smile takes over my face.

She's the one I'm going to miss the most. My anchor in a world that was full of cruelty and uncertainty. The friendship that we have is one not to take for granted.

Ella: I'm on my way to help you get ready for your date. Bringing coffee!

Suri: Hurry up! I need a break.

As soon as I hit send, my dad strolls into my room. "Hey, honey. How's the packing going?"

I can see the slight discoloration under his eyes, so I know he's still not sleeping well. The wrinkles around his eyes and on his forehead have deepened. I worry about him. I worry about leaving him, but he wants me to go. He wants me to be happy.

He was devastated when he heard about Mallory and she used us to get into Brian's organization. He's been going through the stages of grief and right now he's angry. It dulled a little bit when he got the report that her and her associates' bodies had washed up on a beach in Germany.

The relationship between my Dad and I has been strained for a while, but we're working on making it better. When I leave to go to California, I'll be sad to leave him but I think having some distance between us will actually help our relationship. It's not like we won't see each other frequently. He travels there often for work.

I smile at him. "It's going well. The movers are almost done putting everything in the truck except for my bag I packed to travel with."

He places his arms around my shoulders. "That's good, honey. When is your date with Brendan?"

"It's in two hours. Ella is almost here to help me get ready."

"Have fun, Suri. I'll get out of your way and go make a few phone calls. We're still on for breakfast before you leave?"

I nod as he tightens his hold with an awkward half hug. We have years of neglect and hurt sitting between us but even an awkward hug is a start. He releases me and walks out of my room leaving me with my thoughts about everything that's happened in the last few weeks...well, years really.

What if I had never decided to break the rules and follow my heart? Things would be so different. I would still be planning my wedding to Kieran. Brendan and I wouldn't be talking. Mallory may have succeeded in killing me. I'm so happy that I decided to take that chance.

Ella walks in interrupting my what if's. "Here's your coffee. Now let's get you sexy for your date."

I take the next hour and half getting dressed and laughing with my friend. Ella finishes the look off by doing my hair and makeup. I look in the mirror and can't believe it. I don't even look like myself. Ella straightened my curly hair. On my eyes I have smoky eyeshadow and she finished the look with red lips. My makeup is the perfect complement to my strapless eggplant dress.

Putting on the finishing touches, my phone lights up with a text. I whisper to Ella, "He's here."

She smiles at me. "Well, we don't want to make lover boy wait, now do we?"

"No, we better not. He might throw a fit," I laugh and grab my purse.

Making our way down the stairs, we stand in front of the door. Ella gives me a hug and I try not to cry when she whispers, "I'm going to go. Call me when you get to California. I love you, Suri. You are the best person I know and will do great things."

I return her hug, my eyes filled with unshed tears. "I love you too, Ella. Remember you deserve the world."

She turns to head out the garage leaving me. I start to think about all the crap that Brendan and I have been through over the past few years. Starting to fall in love with each other, then being told that we couldn't be together. Wanting to follow our parents orders but hating having to do it. Then taking the chance and telling everyone we wanted to be together. Tomorrow we leave and start our life together, whatever that looks like.

I open the front door and I'm taken aback when I see Henry standing in front of the car instead of Brendan. "Why are you here, Henry?"

He grins and places his finger over his lips. "Shh...it's a secret, Suri. Get in the car, I'll take you to see Brendan."

Wanting to get to Brendan, I comply quickly. We drive into the city and stop in front of Brendan's building.

"Go into the building and take the elevator up to the roof. Brendan will explain everything."

Butterflies start to take flight as I get out of the car. I follow Henry's directions and get in the elevator not sure what to expect when the doors open. Stepping out of the elevator, my jaw drops. Fairy lights fill the rooftop patio making it look like a starry sky. A path of roses leads me away from the elevator and around the corner where all I see is Brendan down on one knee holding a ring. My hands instantly go up to my mouth and tears fill my eyes. When I get close enough, he grabs my hand and the tears start to run down my face.

"Suri, my princess. I have loved you my whole life. I promise to always fight for you, and show you how much I love you. I can't wait to start our new adventure together. Be my wife."

I love how he doesn't ask the question but demands it from me. Not being able to wait any longer, I nod my head and whisper, "Yes!"

Brendan kisses my finger and then slides the ring onto it. It's the most beautiful thing I've ever seen. An emerald, my favorite color, princess cut. Brendan has always been the perfect one for me and now I have the perfect ring for me. When he stands up I jump into his arms, wrap my legs around his hips and give him a huge kiss. When I pull back, I whisper, "I can't wait till you're my husband."

Epilogue

Walking into our beach house in California, a rush of excitement comes over me. My life has changed so much. I have never had a reason to look forward to anything, but now I have everything to look forward to. Taking a deep breath I allow all the possibilities of the future to sweep across my skin.

"Are you ready?" A deep growl interrupts my thoughts.

That voice. That growl. I get that forever. My thighs clench just thinking about him. Looking over my shoulder, I grin at the most handsome man. I know he's watching my thighs. He knows his voice turns me on. I can't fool him. Ignoring the way my clit throbs, I mutter, "Yes, I'm ready."

Beckoning me forward with his finger, my body walks toward him without even thinking. His hand makes its way down my back, grabbing my ass. "You know, princess, I'm so proud of you. This is a brave thing that you're doing."

I just shrug with his praise, "Thank you."

He leans around me and opens the car door for me, but before I can get in, he growls, "I mean it, Suri. Achieving your goals isn't something to scoff at. This is amazing."

Then he leans in and gives me a soft kiss against my lips, but he pulls away before I can deepen the kiss. He smirks....the asshole. He knows exactly what I want.

"You know you will pay for that later," I say with a wink. Climbing into the car, I sit in the seat spreading my legs a bit.

"I'm counting on it," he says near my ear as he leans across to buckle my seatbelt.

Driving toward the city, my hands start to sweat. I try wiping them across my skirt and closing my eyes to count to ten. Brendan's large hand wraps around my thigh. My eyes follow it as he slides it inside my skirt. I feel my underwear move to the side and I let out a sigh. The anticipation of what's going to happen next makes my pussy flood.

Brendan starts to caress my folds, gathering my wetness at my clit. "Does my princess slut want me to help her relax by making her come?"

Words don't come easy for me in these moments so I spread my legs a little to give him more access.

"I need your words, princess."

"Yes, Brendan, make me come," I whisper to him.

Closing my eyes, I try not to think about what I'm going to do in a few minutes. I try not to think at all. I just concentrate on what he's doing and how it feels. All I can hear is my heartbeat and his voice. "That's right, be a good little princess, and just enjoy what I'm doing to you."

Without even thinking, I feel my legs spreading even more, trying to get Brendan to touch the spot that I need the most. I feel one finger enter me as the heel of his palm grazes my clit. My hips jut up needing more. "Do you need me to fill my whore up more?"

Before I can answer, he puts a second finger in and I gasp. "Fuck, princess, you are so tight for me."

Then he puts a third finger in me moving them in and out. I can hear how wet I am. Concentrating on that sound and the pressure from his hand on my clit makes my pussy start to contract around his fingers. "Yes, princess. You're doing so good taking my fingers like that."

I get even wetter with every word he says. You would think I would be embarrassed by how his words affect me, but I don't have it in me. He's proven time and time again how much he loves everything about my body.

Suddenly my whole body tightens up and all I see is stars behind my eyes. When I come down from my high, Brendan takes his fingers from me and puts them in his mouth. I feel empty instantly and miss the way I stretch around him. He grins because he knows what he does to me, "Mmm...Princess, you taste so fucking sweet. Do you feel better?"

"Yes, I needed that," I mutter shyly. Brendan doesn't say anything else to me, but he knows exactly how to handle me and my anxiety before every book reading. I've done this a few times before but I still get really nervous and Brendan just allows me to do my thing.

We walk back toward the back of the bookstore hand in hand, not lingering too long because then I might talk myself out of it. I need to be there for those who love my book and the stories I tell. And I know I'll always have Brendan at my side to help me through the tough spots. We've had our share and made it through...together.

"Suri!" I hear as soon as I walk into the bookstore. I turn toward the familiar voice.

"Ella?"

Running toward her, we wrap each other in a tight hug. It's been six months since the last time I saw her and I've missed her like crazy. "I can't believe you're here."

"You should thank your man here," she says as she nudges Brendan with her elbow. My jaw drops turning back toward him. "You did this?"

Shrugging, he says, "You've been saying you missed Ella so I brought her here."

I stare at him for a bit. "You are the best. I love you."

He grins at me while wrapping his arm around my waist pulling me closer. He whispers in my ear, "You can thank me properly later, Princess."

My face turns red and I clear my throat at the same time Ella makes a gagging noise. "Um...Ella, you want to sit with Brendan while I do the reading?"

"Of course! I can't wait to see you in action. I've read the book and it's so freaking good."

All three of us start to head to the reading room in the bookstore when the crowd starts to clap. I'll never get used to that. I feel my face flushing and it's so hot in here. But these fans are the reason I wanted to write my book and they are all here for me. Crazy, right?

Leaving Brendan and Ella to find their seats, I make my way to the podium. Tapping the microphone, the crowd went silent. Standing tall, I address the room, "Thank you for coming. I'm always shocked with how many people have read my books and are here to support me."

I look down in the front row, and my eyes connect with Brendan. My life hasn't always been easy and I know what it's like to be lonely. But with him by my side I know I will never be alone again. I push back the happy tears and begin, "This story holds a special place in my heart, and you can't imagine how it makes me feel that so many of you can connect with it too. Now let's get to the reading. Chapter One: Meeting the Love of her Life."

***

Want to read about how Brendan surprises Suri for their wedding? Grab it here in this bonus scene.

A Note from the Author

Thank you so much for going on this journey with me. This book has been so much fun. When I went into writing this story, I was originally going to keep Suri and Brendan apart longer. I will tell you that these two were not having it. I woke many times in the middle of the night with the whispers from Brendan that they needed to be together. The pull between them was just too great. I hope you enjoyed this book, and my version of The Frog Prince. Please share Suri and Brendan's love story with your friends.

This book is the second book in an interconnected standalone series. Each book will be based off of a Brothers Grimm fairy tale.

Wondering about Zeev and his story? Find out in the first book Red.

Remember Ella, Suri's best friend? Her story Midnight Blue will be coming February 2024.

***

STALK ME ON SOCIAL MEDIA:

Website: www.nicholeruschelle.com

Facebook Private Reader Group:

Nichole's Romance Realm

IG: AuthorNicholeRuschelle

TikTok: AuthorNicholeRuschelle

Acknowledgements

Making time to write is not an easy feat. I want to thank my husband because without him I would not be able to find the time to get these stories out.

To my girls, it fills my heart with so much pride when you tell people that your mom writes books. I've never been the type of person who seeks approval from others, but having the approval of you girls is everything I never realized I needed. We will see if you still approve when you're older, and you actually can read what I write.

A huge thank you to my friend and photographer Katie from Cadwallader Photography. The photo for this cover is perfection. Most importantly, thank you for putting up with all the nonsense you have to deal with from me including an excessive amount of voice and text messages. I would not be able to get through this process without all of your support. I'm so happy that we met over a romance novel in our daughters' swim class.

Karen from Utterly Unashamed, thank you for going through the editing process with me. I loved learning and for you giving me things to think about while writing. I can't wait to work on future projects with you.

Megan, thank you again for handling my frantic text messages and proofreading the book quickly.

Thank you to all the readers who are taking a chance on a new author and spreading the word about my books. Ya'll are the heroes in my story and I love all of you for it.

About the Author

Nichole Ruschelle lives in Texas with her husband, two daughters and her zoo of animals. She is an author who loves to write fairytales with a twist. You can always expect her stories to have an alpha guy who falls hard for his independent leading lady. In her free time Nichole can usually be found reading romance novels off of her Kindle. If she isn't reading, then she is usually found sitting at the pool or outside of pottery class while her kids do their activities.

Made in the USA
Las Vegas, NV
03 February 2025